# *Crazy*
# *Stupid*
# *Love*

A *Crazy Love* Novel

# MELISSA TOPPEN

MELISSA TOPPEN


Copyright © 2016 Melissa Toppen

**Crazy Stupid Love**

Written by Melissa Toppen

# TABLE OF CONTENTS

*Sometimes falling in love isn't just crazy, it's downright stupid…*

*Embrace the madness.*

# Prologue

## **Decklan**

Screams, that's all I can hear. The shrill cries of a woman that pierces my ears with so much intensity the ringing in my head becomes nearly unbearable, the pressure between my temples threatening to explode at any moment.

Distant voices filter into the chaos of white noise and random muffled tones seem to seep their way in from a distant place. I don't recognize any of them. Except one...the screaming woman, her I know.

My body becomes weightless, lifting from the ground as if to float away.

Am I dying?

Am I already dead?

I can't be...there's too much pain. It

radiates from everywhere. I can feel it coursing through my limbs, demanding to be felt.

Please make it stop.

I just want it to go away.

I can't take it.

It's too much.

Then I remember...

My eyes dart open, searching frantically. He's here. He's right here.

Where is he?

"Conner," I manage to say, but my voice is broken and not audible over the bustle of unrecognizable people that seem to close in around me.

"Where's Conner?" I try again, this time my voice managing to catch the attention of a man next to me, his face unrecognizable through my blurred, distorted vision.

"He's responding." I hear the voice say to another.

"We've got you, son." Another voice.

"Conner," I demand more forcefully, still too disoriented to know who I am speaking to.

"We've got you." I hear again.

Why is no one answering me?

Where are they taking me?

My mind may not be able to process what is happening but somehow it already seems to know. Conner's gone... I just know it. I can feel it; like losing a part of myself.

I want to scream, demand that I see him, but I'm a prisoner to this body. This damaged broken body that has no fight left in it.

I silently close my eyes and let the darkness take me.

It's where I belong.

It's where I've always belonged.

# Chapter One

## **<u>Kimber</u>**

I knew I shouldn't have come here tonight. I don't know why I let my roommate and her crazy best friend drag me all the way to Portland, let alone dress me in this tight little cocktail dress that makes it feel difficult to breathe normally. I guess it's my feeble attempt to feel like I'm a part of something; to fit in. But now as I sit here watching the two girls grind on any man within a ten-foot radius of them, it's blindingly clear that fitting in is not something I am doing.

It's been nearly two months since I moved to Oregon, and I still feel like such an outsider. Even still, I do my best not to seem too out of place sitting at a round high-top table all by myself in the back of a hopping bar, sipping virgin strawberry daiquiris like I am *not* the biggest loser in the world.

To say a bar named *Deviants* is out of my comfort zone is a major understatement. With dark walls, wild lights, and the most elaborate looking glass bar, I can honestly say I have never stepped foot inside of somewhere even remotely similar to this. Places like this don't exist in the tiny town I grew up in, at least not that I was ever aware of. Of course, I had blinders on for most of my life, thanks to my overprotective parents who kept me, from what I am now learning, quite sheltered.

It wasn't an easy decision leaving my home in West Virginia, let alone moving to the opposite side of the country, but I knew if I wanted any chance of becoming my own person I had to do it.

My parents' were furious  and while things are still not okay with us, we are at least on speaking terms again.  Of course, they refused to pay for even one dime of my tuition. Luckily I worked my butt off in high school and graduated at the top of my class, earning myself quite a hefty Art scholarship to The University of Oregon. A far cry from the legal or medical degree my parents' dreamed I would pursue.

I shake my head and hold up my drink

when my roommate Harlee waves for me to join her on the dance floor. She rolls her eyes and throws me an annoyed glare but is quickly distracted when a dark-haired man steps up behind her and begins rubbing his crotch into her backside. I can't help but cringe slightly. I don't see the fun in having random sweaty strangers rub up all over you like that.

"Could you be any lamer?" Angel, Harlee's wild-haired best friend startles me with her sudden presence.

"I'm not lame." I huff. "I'm people watching." I take a long sip of my icy drink, pushing my dark blonde waves behind my shoulders as I straighten my posture.

"Like I said, lame." She jumps slightly when a man who looks to be at least thirty slides in behind her, setting a beer and a multicolored shot in front of her despite the fact that she's not legally old enough to drink; none of us are.

Giving me a wicked smile, she raises the shot glass to her lips and tips it back, draining the liquid in seconds.

"Delicious," she hisses, wiping her lips with the back of her hand before turning in the man's arms.

Locking her hands around the back of his neck, she pulls him into a kiss so heated it makes me blush slightly just being near them.

"Get a room," I mumble under my

breath, turning my eyes away from the indecency taking place just to my right.

I have only been around Angel a handful of times, but I have her pretty figured out at this point. She's not all that picky when it comes to men and loves being the center of attention. Everywhere she goes she feeds off of it.

If her black hair with bright blue streaks doesn't give it away, her short skirts and barely-there shirts definitely prove that she likes turning heads. She has most definitely turned the head of the man now lapping his tongue up her neck reminding me more of a dog than an actual human being.

Harlee isn't much different though she tends to be a little more subtle about it. Instead of crazy colors, she sports almost platinum blonde hair that hangs nearly to her waist, and her preferred outfits of choice are tight little tube dresses or yoga pants that leave very little to the imagination.

Either way, I couldn't be more different than the two girls I let drag me nearly an hour and a half from campus on a Saturday night. Truth be told, I have yet to really meet anyone who doesn't value the very same things they do. I most definitely feel like I am in the minority. I guess it just stems back to how I was raised.

Don't get me wrong, a part of me wants

to lash out, go completely crazy and just live life like these girls do. I just don't know that I have it in me. I'm trying. I'm trying to push myself out of my comfort zone, out of the contained little bubble my parents' kept me prisoner in for so long, but even when I do it seems like I just end up doing exactly what I'm doing now.

"Why don't you join us, Kimber?" Angel leans forward and snags her beer from the table, taking a long drink before turning her gaze back to me.

"I'm good," I insist, realizing very quickly that I am going to have to be the one to drive Angel's car home as she lifts the bottle to her lips again.

"Suit yourself." She grabs the hand of the man behind her and bounces off towards the dance floor, towing him with her.

She's gone no more than sixty seconds when I look up and lock eyes with an approaching male, a sleazy looking twenty-something who quickly slides up next to me.

"You look like you could use a drink," he says, and he's not the first person to approach me tonight saying almost the exact same thing.

"I'm good." I smile politely, trying not to tense when he leans in closer.

"Oh come on, honey. Let me buy you a *real* drink," he insists. He skirts his hand along my lower back as he steps in closer and nods towards my near empty daiquiri.

"Really. I'm good here," I insist, leaning to the right trying to put a little distance between us.

"You sure? Looks to me like you could use some loosening up." He breathes, his hot beer-scented breath dancing across my face.

"If you'll excuse me," I say as I slide from the stool, my sudden movement causing the man to topple forward slightly. "I think my friend needs me." I don't look back as I make a v-line towards the front door, hoping the man doesn't follow me.

Weaving in and out of the various people that crowd the room, I let out a loud exhale the moment the fresh night air fills my lungs. Stepping to the edge of the sidewalk, I slide down onto the curb, careful to keep my backside covered in this tiny dress as I do. Stretching my legs out in front of me, I ignore the multiple conversations taking place to my right where several people have gathered to smoke.

I take another deep inhale and let it out slowly, looking to my left when I spot someone leaning against a motorcycle parked on the side of the road. My eyes land on a pair of black boots first then dark ripped jeans as they climb higher. A tight fitted V-neck t-shirt reveals rippling muscles below the thin fabric and causes me to take a shaky breath as my eyes continue upward.

The moment the man's face comes into view all the air leaves my body. His full lips wrap around a cigarette held loosely in his hand and he takes a hard drag, smoke billowing from his mouth seconds later.

I'm immediately drawn to his wild sexy hair, the way the dark blond strands are pushed to the side haphazardly with a large chunk falling in front of one of his eyes. His jaw is strong and prominent even hidden below the mass of short dark stubble that covers his incredibly handsome face. I would guess him in his mid to late twenties.

He takes another drag of his cigarette, completely oblivious to the fact that I have not taken my eyes off him. He stares blankly ahead, his features drawn and hard like he's deep in thought.

I don't know what it is about him, but just looking at him rattles me. It's not his looks, the attraction is obvious, it's more about his presence; how even though he's standing completely alone he seems to command the very world that surrounds him.

He lets out another smoky exhale before dropping his cigarette to the ground, crushing the burning tip under the sole of his boot. Flipping his eyes to the side, the moment they meet mine I feel like I have been transported to some alternate reality; the ground beneath me seeming to shift on its very axis. He's even more breathtaking from the front.

I may not be promiscuous like Harlee or Angel, but that doesn't mean I'm immune to men, it just takes a lot more than a look to get me all riled up, or it usually does anyway. Something about sitting in this man's gaze has me feeling a variation of things I'm not certain I have ever really felt before; lust being the most prominent feeling of them all.

His deep gray eyes study me for a long moment, the air so thick between us I feel like I might suffocate under the weight. I open my mouth, feeling like I need to say something. Before I can even muster up the courage to speak he breaks the connection, turning his eyes forward as he pushes away from the bike and heads back inside the bar.

I sit glued to the sidewalk for several long seconds before reality seems to resurface. What was that all about? Trying to shake off the feeling the sexy stranger has left me with, I decide it's time get back inside and find my friends so I can get the hell out of here.

The moment I re-enter *Deviants,* I head straight towards the dance floor catching the eyes of Harlee as I approach who throws her hands up in excitement at the sight of me.

"It's about time, bitch!" she slurs, wrapping an arm around the back of my neck.

"Can we go?" I push up on my tiptoes and yell into her ear over the music pounding from the speakers just feet from us.

"Why?" She pulls back and hits me with sad puppy dog eyes.

While Harlee may be a bit of a wild child, she also has a huge heart. I know if I insist on leaving, she will agree; even if it is reluctantly. She's gone way out of her way to make me feel welcome and to include me, and I know she wouldn't go through the trouble if she didn't care.

"It's nearly midnight," I shout, tapping my wrist to indicate the time.

"Thirty more minutes," she mouths, pouting out her lip for good measure.

Not wanting to be the person who ruins her good time, I sigh and nod, knowing that if I want any chance at reinventing myself, I'm going to have to suck it up every now and again and deal with situations I don't want to be in. I never dreamed how different life would be in Oregon versus West Virginia. It's almost like living on a different planet entirely.

A wide smile cracks across her pretty face, and she pulls me into a tight hug, causing me to have to turn my head to avoid my face going directly into her chest. Harlee towers over me, standing around 5'9" which puts her about a full head taller than me.

Managing to squiggle out of her grasp, I point towards the bar, mouthing that I'm going to be there. She nods and then spins towards Angel, throwing her hands up above her head as she resumes bouncing around the dance floor.

I keep my gaze down as I cross towards the sleek glass bar that stretches almost the entire length of the left side wall, purposely wanting to avoid another encounter with the gray eyes that still have my stomach twisted in all sorts of knots.

I slide into the first open stool I can find, which happens to be squeezed between a large bald man and an older woman clearly trying to appear younger than she actually is. I wave my hand trying to catch the attention of the bartender who appears to be looking in every direction but mine.

He crosses the length of the bar sliding drinks to various customers as he goes. I can't help but be impressed by his skills. It's almost like he was bred to tend bar, as ridiculous as that sounds.

He's an attractive man: dark hair that's shaved underneath and a little longer on top, wearing ripped jeans and a fitted t-shirt that clings to his clearly muscular body, and just the right amount of facial hair covering his handsome face; pretty much the exact opposite of my type. The type I usually date anyway; well the *one* I dated.

I guess considering I have only ever dated Garrett, I can't say I really have a usual type. Just the type my parents' deemed acceptable. I guess that's why I spent three years of my life dating a man I'm not even sure I liked.

I make one more attempt to snag the bartender's attention before finally settling back into my stool, deciding to wait until he comes my way to ask for a glass of water. Pulling my cell phone out of the small purse draped over my shoulder, I unlock the screen and double check my messages, sighing loudly when I see Garrett has called twice despite the fact that I have asked him repeatedly to give me some time.

Locking the phone I shove it forcefully back into my bag, not feeling up to dealing with his antics at the present moment.

"Let me guess, your boyfriend is upset that you're out with friends." A smooth deep voice pulls my attention forward.

I freeze the moment my eyes lock on the gray ones that held me so completely captive outside just a few short minutes ago. I take in a ragged inhale, not prepared for how incredible he looks looming just across the bar from me.

I knew he was attractive, but seeing him like this— shrouded under the dim lights—

he's more than just another handsome face. There is something so haunted behind those incredible eyes.

It doesn't take a genius to figure out that this man is trouble. It seeps from his very pores like an invisible warning label. He's exactly the type of man I know with complete certainty would break any girl who was foolish enough to offer him her heart.

"I... Um..." I stutter over my words, feeling the heat rush to my cheeks. "I don't have a boyfriend." I breathe, the words barely audible over the loud music and busy chatter of the crowd.

"No?" He cocks his head to the side, his eyes narrowing in on my face. "Surprising." He sets an empty glass in front of me, proceeding to fill it with ice and then water.

"How did you..." I start, but he doesn't allow me to finish.

"You've been drinking virgin daiquiris all night, and from what I can tell, you're dying to get the hell out of here. I took a guess." He gestures to the water.

I try to seem completely unaffected by the fact that he's clearly been watching me, at least enough to know what I've been drinking. Honestly, just the thought causes my stomach to twist in knots and sends my heart galloping inside of my chest.

"Good guess," I observe, lifting the glass

hesitantly to my lips before taking a small drink, just needing a reason not to speak considering how flustered I feel.

"You work here?" I ask, slowly lowering the glass back to the bar, trying to figure out how in the world I would have missed him behind the bar considering I have spent a good deal of my night watching the people that were crowding it.

"No, I just randomly pretend I do so I can talk to beautiful women," he says, tilting his head back on a light laugh when he sees I take him at his word. "I'm kidding." He shakes his head, his smile revealing perfectly straight white teeth.

"Oh." I flush again, embarrassed by how gullible I must seem but even more affected by the fact that he just implied he finds me beautiful.

"Yo, Deck." The bartender steps up next to the man in front of me, resting his hand on his shoulder as he leans in to say something under his breath.

Immediately his gray eyes dart towards the stage where the D.J. is set up, scouring the crowd before apparently finding what he's looking for.

"You'll have to excuse me..." He turns his attention back to me the moment the bartender walks away.

"Kimber," I answer, realizing he's

waiting for my name.

"Kimber," he says the name slowly, smiling with the way it flows from his lips. "It was nice talking to you, Kimber."

"You, too," I say, not getting a chance to say anymore before he's heading out from behind the bar, immediately disappearing into the crowd.

I turn my eyes to the left just in time to see Harlee skipping towards me, spinning mid-hop managing to bump into a few annoyed people in the process before finally reaching me.

"Best night ever!" she exclaims, dropping her arm over my shoulder. "Angel, girl let's get this show on the road," she screams behind her, moments before Angel appears.

My stomach immediately drops when I realize they are ready to leave. I was all but begging my way out of here twenty minutes ago, and now the last thing I want to do is leave. I didn't even get a chance to ask him his name, other than hearing the bartender refer to him as Deck.

The weird thing is I can't figure out why I even care. It's not like I plan on ever coming back here again. Though the idea of doing just that definitely crosses my mind as I follow Angel and Harlee out of the bar, unable to resist glancing behind me one last time in hopes of catching just one more glimpse of the man who quite literally rendered me speechless.

# Chapter Two

## **Decklan**

"Seriously dude, again with this shit." I kick Gavin's leg nudging him awake. "How many times have I asked you to take your shit home?" I hover over him as he fights to pry his eyes open, the brunette passed out across his chest not even budging. "This is our place of business, not a fucking motel."

"Drank too much. Couldn't drive." He finally manages to get his eyes open enough to peer down at the naked woman on top of him.

"Then you should have put her ass in a cab and crashed upstairs," I say, referring to the apartment above the bar that has been my home for the past four years.

I moved up there after me and Gavin sunk every dime we had into buying this bar, unable to afford the lease on the building and a place to live at the same time. Of course, back then it was a complete dump. Nothing like the hot spot Gavin and I have managed to turn it into. I could have moved out a long time ago, but honestly, it's not a bad space, and I like being so close in case anything happens.

"And crash on that lumpy ass couch of yours." Gavin stretches, sliding the woman from his chest as he pushes into a sitting position.

"And this is any better? You realize how many nasty fuckers walk on this floor?"

"Yeah, but at least down here I have something to make the sleeping arrangements more accommodating. Man, she's out," he says, gesturing to the woman now lying face down on the floor. "Besides, it's not like you haven't done it before."

"Fucked in here, yes. Slept on this nasty ass floor, fuck no." I shake my head. "Shay hasn't even cleaned yet. You're literally laying in filth."

"Just the way I like it." He smirks, nudging the woman next to him. "Hey. Hey." He repeats, shaking her by the shoulder.

She lets out a small groan but makes no attempt to move.

"Hey." He continues shaking. "You gotta go..." He pauses. "Fuck, dude, I don't know her name." He laughs, scratching the side of his head.

"I don't give a fuck what her name is; get her the fuck out of here," I demand, stepping past them to slide behind the bar and gather the money from the previous night's business.

Laying the cash on the counter, I immediately grab a lowball glass and the nearest whiskey bottle, pouring the liquid to the rim before putting the bottle back. Raising the glass to my lips, I take a deep inhale and then pour the contents down my throat. The burn is horrific but just what I need; something to dull me a bit.

Waking up is always my least favorite part of the day. That's when everything comes flooding back. It gets easier as the day progresses and I have time to numb it away, but then the next morning it returns full force, same as the last.

Deciding I'm going to need one more, I fill the glass again, my eyes following Gavin as he half carries the still drunk girl towards the bar.

"You could fucking help me," he grunts, sliding the woman onto a bar stool.

She immediately leans forward, groaning loudly as she rests her forehead against the bar in front of her.

"I'm not the one that stuck my dick in her." I shake my head before lifting the glass back to my lips, the second drink going down much smoother than the first.

"Whatever dick. Can you at least call a cab?" He slides onto the stool next to her, lifting my glass to his nose. "Starting off with the hard shit today, that can't be good," he observes.

"I promised Mom I would meet her and Trey for lunch. I don't know why I even fucking agreed to it. I know exactly how it's going to go." I sigh, considering pouring a third drink but quickly deciding against it. I do have to drive after all.

"Then why did you?" he questions, knowing how difficult the relationship between me and my older brother has been over the past few years.

"Because she's my mother, one of the only people in my family that doesn't treat me like I'm just a piece of fucking scum the world would be better off without. At least for my sake, she pretends not to feel that way." The thought has me pouring another drink despite my decision to call it at two.

The moment the liquid seers my throat I feel my nerves start to calm; the potency of the whiskey making everything a bit more tolerable.

"So are you going to tell me who that girl

was, the one I saw you staring at all night? I gotta say I'm surprised she wasn't doing the walk of shame out of your apartment this morning." He laughs, signally that I pour him a shot from the bottle still sitting in front of me.

"One, it wasn't like that. I was just really fucking intrigued by what someone like her was doing here. She seemed so out of place. Two, you know I don't let women sleep over," I say, sitting a clean glass in front of him before filling it with whiskey.

"Well I don't know why it *wasn't* like that; that bitch was hot." He smirks, causing me to have to swallow down my knee-jerk reaction to slam his head down onto the bar.

I can't justify the reaction, nor do I have the mental capacity right now to even really think about it. She may have been stunning but also entirely out of my league. I know the difference between a fuckable woman and one that is simply off limits. She's way too innocent to handle me, and I don't have the time to worry about staining a perfect canvas. I don't need any more guilt on my fucking conscience.

"Whatever dude." I shake off the thought, grabbing my cell from my pocket before punching in the phone number for the local cab company. It takes me less than thirty seconds to secure a car for Gavin's half passed out one-nighter. "They'll be here in ten," I say, sliding the phone back into my jeans before collecting the cash on the bar.

"Thanks, dude."

"Whatever. Just make sure you're here to let Shay in so he can get this place back into shape for tonight. And please, for the love of fuck, take a shower. You fucking stink," I say, exiting the bar before Gavin can say anymore.

****

The vibration of my motorcycle beneath me soothes my nerves during the long two-hour ride to Springfield. I weave in and out of traffic, the visor of my helmet left open so I can feel the wind whip against my face.

It's not often that I get to take my bike out for such long trips and I have to admit, while I'm dreading the destination, I am rather enjoying the ride.

While the October temperatures have dropped into the sixties over the past couple of weeks, I don't feel even the slightest chill. The whiskey is still running warm in my veins despite the loss of its effects on my mind.

Pulling my bike into a side street parking spot, I power off the engine and slide the helmet from my head, running a hand through my tangled hair. Pulling out a cigarette, I light it and take a deep inhale, loving the way the smoke fills my lungs, the burn that engulfs my chest. Taking another long drag, I look around, taking in the scenery. The area packed with college aged kids carrying laptop bags and books, no doubt heading towards the nearest coffee shop to congregate.

Having grown up just ten minutes from Eugene, I'm used to the atmosphere. The University of Oregon draws in a younger crowd that dominates this part of town; primarily the reason why I avoid coming out this way. Well that, and the fact that I have no desire to return home or to relive the demons that haunt this place.

I relive that same hell every morning just by opening my eyes. I don't need any additional reminders telling me what I lost. What I broke.

Climbing off my motorcycle, I take one last drag before dropping the cigarette to the ground, stomping it out with my boot. Latching the helmet to the handlebars, I straighten my black leather jacket before sliding on my aviator sunglasses. I'll do anything I can to conceal my identity. Not that there's anyone around who knows or gives a fuck who I am, but I don't even like risking it.

I spot my mother sitting at a round table in the outdoor patio area at *Lovett's*, her favorite little diner, the menu just inches from her face. Her blonde hair is shorter than the last time I saw her and peppered with more gray than I remember. I have to remind myself that it's been almost a year, since last Christmas to be exact.

Visions of that night flood through my mind. Trey, the shit he fucking spewed, the way my mom cried. It was almost as bad as that night with Conner. I shake off the memory, taking a deep breath as I approach her.

"Mother," I say, pulling out the chair next to her.

She immediately lowers the menu and hits me with gentle eyes and a sweet smile.

"Oh, my sweet boy. Look at you," she says, gesturing for me to sit. "You look so... grown up." She pats the back of my hand when I settle down next to her, my eyes immediately falling to the only other chair placed at the small round table.

"Tell me, how are you?" she asks, ignoring my obvious tension.

"I'm good. Things are good."

Lies. Lies. Lies.

What I really should be saying is that I'm a fucking alcoholic who fucks everything that moves just to feel something other than my own pain.

"And Gavin? How are things at the bar?" She does her best to fill the silence.

"The bar's good. Gavin is, well Gavin." I shrug and she laughs, knowing Gavin really well from our childhood.

With as much as he stayed at my house, hell we were practically brothers. Not to mention that his parents took me in for the last half of my senior year until I graduated and could get the fuck out of here.

"Business is good then?" She pulls my attention from the past back to her.

"Really well." I stop, turning my gaze to the waitress when she steps up next to my mother.

"Can I get you something to drink Sir?" she asks, her eyes immediately widening when they land on me.

Well, fuck me. If it isn't the sweet little thing from last night, only she looks much different in the bright afternoon sun; almost angelic. Instead of sporting a tight little dress that she clearly wasn't comfortable wearing, she's more casual today; wearing a long flowing white top and dark skinny jeans, her long blonde waves pulled back into a messy bun.

"It's Kimber, isn't it?" I say, smiling when her lips part in surprise.

"Hi." She seems to regain her composure. "It's nice to see you again." She takes another long pause. "Can I get you something to drink?" She nervously tucks a stray curl behind her ear, the movement causing my stomach muscles to clench tightly.

She's so fucking innocent. So pure. I can think of a hundred ways I could corrupt that tight little body of hers. A hundred different positions I could fuck her in. Just the thought of her screaming my name makes my groin twitch.

Clearing my throat, I realize I haven't responded.

"What do you have on tap?" I ask, ignoring my mother's gaze and the look of disapproval that is surely etched across her face.

Kimber nervously rambles off a list she clearly is still trying to memorize, going back twice to add to the non-domestic beer list before I finally just settle on a Guinness. She smiles nervously and walks away, my gaze immediately falling to her backside when she does. It takes everything in me to keep my posture casual when every muscle in my body seems to tighten.

Thankfully I'm still wearing my sunglasses because my mother doesn't seem to notice my mental stray. She picks up the conversation exactly where we left off, asking more about the bar, clearly just trying to take an interest in what I'm doing when she probably couldn't care less.

I catch sight of Kimber just minutes

later when she reappears onto the patio, a large frosted beer mug in her hand. When she leans over and sets it next to me, I get a waft of her scent; vanilla with a hint of something sweet that I can't quite pinpoint; coconut maybe. I breathe in deeply, letting the intoxicating smell linger in my nostrils for a moment longer. Yes, definitely coconut. It's a light smell, refreshing, and so very fitting for her.

"Is there anything else I can get for you or are you still waiting for the rest of your party?" She turns her attention to my mother.

"We will wait." She starts but then retracts when she catches sight of Trey making his way towards the table. "Scratch that. There he is," she says more to Trey than Kimber.

"Water with lemon," Trey instructs Kimber without even batting an eye in her direction. I don't know why but the action makes me want to shove his fucking face into the table.

She nods and quickly exits without a word.

"Decklan. You're looking, well..." He takes a long pause. "The same," he says judgingly, his eyes taking in my appearance.

"We can't all be perfect now can we?" I give him a tight smile and gesture to his black sweater and khaki pants.

Fuck. With his short side swept hair and

that ridiculous getup, he looks like he just stepped out of a prep school magazine. Fucking tool.

"Well it wouldn't hurt some of us to try," he says, kissing mom on the cheek before taking the seat between us to my left.

"You got something you want to fucking say?" I spout, feeling already too on edge for his bullshit.

"Oh, I've got a lot of things I'd like to say, little brother."

"Then fucking say it, Trey." I clasp my hands together to keep myself from lunging in his direction.

"Now boys." My mother immediately interferes when Kimber reappears at my brother's side, setting his water on the table.

"Ridiculous," Trey adds on, fueling my temper to near its breaking point. "It should have been you." He mumbles under his breath, breaking the last tiny thread holding me in place.

"You think I don't wish that every fucking day, Trey? You think I don't wish it had been me?" I growl, my voice carrying far enough to draw the attention of the other patrons dining on the patio.

"Decklan. Trey." My mother's voice turns firm. "That's enough."

The moment I catch sight of Kimber still standing next to the table, a look of what I can only describe as fear across her pretty face, I feel my temper give a bit. Hell, I almost feel bad for nearly losing it in front of her. Though I'm not entirely sure why I care.

"You're right. I'm sorry." Trey speaks directly to my mother, but I keep my eyes locked firmly on Kimber who seems to shrink a bit under my gaze.

"I'm going to give you all a few minutes," She finally says, backing slowly away from the table before quickly spinning on her heel and disappearing back inside.

"Can we please just get through one meal as a family?" My mother pulls my attention back to her. "Decklan, we never see you anymore. I just want to enjoy an afternoon with both of my children."

"Of course, Mother," Trey speaks again.

Fucking kiss ass.

"Sorry, Mom," I grumble, lifting the beer to my lips, draining the contents of my glass in a matter of seconds.

# Chapter Three

## **<u>Kimber</u>**

What are the odds?

What are the odds that out of all the restaurants between here and Portland he would walk into the one that I just happen to work at? Standing just inside the wall that separates the indoor dining area from the outdoor patio, I chance a peek in the direction of the man I now know as Decklan.

*Decklan.*

Even his name is sexy as sin.

My God, this man is all kinds of gorgeous, and of course, I'm fumbling around like a babbling idiot, unable to keep my thoughts straight when he's staring at me through his aviator sunglasses. I don't have to see his brilliant gray eyes through the dark lenses to feel the intensity of his stare behind them.

Taking a deep breath, I make my way back out towards the table. The occupants seem much calmer now that they have food to replace the need for conversation; well, everyone except Decklan who has chosen a liquid diet for this afternoon, now on his third beer.

I can't help but wonder if he always drinks this much or if it's the current situation he finds himself in which clearly isn't a pleasant one. From my frequent trips to their table, I have learned at least a couple of things.

The woman is his mother, that much is clear. Not only have I heard him refer to her as such, but he also looks a great deal like her. The other man is his older brother, Trey I believe. I only know this because I overheard him call Decklan 'little brother' so that left out a lot of the guess work. Though based on their appearance I never would have guessed it.

Decklan is all leather and ripped jeans, rugged and impossibly sexy, while his brother looks like an uppity frat boy. His dark hair is combed nicely to the side, and his face is free of any hair. He's an attractive enough man but has nothing on Decklan.

Either way, it's clear to see that neither man particularly cares for the other. From the bits and pieces I've gathered, I'm guessing something big happened between them and it's not that they simply don't get along.

I can feel Decklan's eyes on me before I even make it to the table. I try my best to keep my face relaxed and not give away just how affected I actually am by this fact.

"Can I get anyone anything?" I ask, positioning myself between Decklan's brother and mother once I reach the table.

"No, dear. I think we're fine." Decklan's mother is the first to respond, giving me a sweet smile as she slides her near empty salad plate to the side.

"We'll take the checks please," Trey speaks next, his voice clipped.

"Of course." I nod, clearing away their empty plates, avoiding Decklan's gaze as I do.

I don't know why I feel so on edge around him. Okay, so he's good looking. It's not like I haven't seen an attractive man before. There's just something about him, I can't explain it.

It takes me a good five minutes to get the system to cooperate and print out their checks. Having only worked here for three weeks, I'm still struggling a bit with the finicky computer systems they use.

When I finally make it back out onto the

patio, the dynamic has completely changed. Decklan's mother is crying softly, and Decklan looks as though he's ready to kill someone; his face contorted in anger as he glares at Trey across the table.

Not sure what to do, I silently deposit the payment books onto the table and quietly slip away. The tension is so heavy I can feel the weight of it just by being in close proximity.

I glance outside over the next several minutes while still tending to my customers that are seated indoors, but I can't really get a feel of what exactly is going on. After delivering food to two different tables, I decide to head back out and collect their money.

My stomach sinks slightly when I realize that the only people remaining at the table are Decklan's mother and brother.

"I'm sorry about all the commotion," she says, wiping her damp cheeks with her napkin.

"Don't apologize, Mom. It's not your fault." Trey reassures her, patting the back of her hand.

"Are you sure there's nothing else I can get for you?" I ask, eager to escape the awkwardness of a clearly emotional situation.

"No, dear. Thank you." She gives me a weak smile.

I nod, turning to collect the payment

books from the table before heading back inside.

Having paid in cash, the moment I leave the table she stands, collecting her purse, exiting the patio just moments later with Trey at her side.

Letting out a slow exhale, I turn my attention to cashing out each check, trying to focus on something other than my disappointment with how quickly Decklan left. I don't know what I expected. I guess I hoped maybe...hell, I don't know what I was hoping for.

Shaking my head, I flip open the last payment book to find Decklan's check inside but no money along with it. Confused, I glance back towards the table thinking maybe he left the cash there but immediately freeze when I realize he has reclaimed his seat at the table.

Swallowing down the sudden lump in my throat, I head slowly back outside, more nervous now than I have been since he arrived because now I don't have the buffer of his family being with him.

"Sorry. I thought you left so I picked this up," I say, sitting the payment book back onto the table in front of him.

"What time do you get off work?" he asks, completely bypassing my statement.

"What?" The word falls from my lips in confusion, but I quickly recover. "Um, here in the next few minutes," I say, doing my best to seem as casual as possible. "I have to wait for the rest of my tables to cash out."

He nods his head slowly as if processing the information. "In that case, I think I'll have one more." He gives me a slow smirk that makes my knees tremble slightly below my weight.

"Oh, okay," I say, not sure why what time I get off work plays a factor in him staying for another drink.

Confusion swarms my mind as I try to figure out exactly what is happening right now. And while I am a bit scared at the possibility that maybe he wants to hang out when I get off, the thought also sends an excitement through me that is nearly impossible to contain.

Picking the payment book up, I return just moments later with his fourth beer and his new check. He gives me a slow nod, his gaze following me as I set the glass down in front of him.

"You're not from around here, are you?" He cocks his head to the side as if trying to figure something out.

"Am I that obvious?" I blush slightly, not entirely able to control the flood of all the emotions I'm currently experiencing.

"Let me guess, Indiana?" He crosses his arms casually in front of himself as he relaxes back into his chair.

"West Virginia." A small laugh manages to escape my lips at his expression.

"Close enough." He gives me an amused smile, the action making him so incredibly sexy I can barely stifle the moan that seems to work its way into my throat.

"I take it you *are* from here?" I force myself to speak.

"Is it that obvious?" He repeats my question back to me.

"Kind of." I can't contain my wide smile when he leans his head back on a deep laugh. "Well, I should get back to work," I say, gesturing towards the indoor dining room. "Is there anything else I can get for you?"

"Not at the moment." He gives me a wicked smile and slides his aviators down just far enough that his gray eyes meet mine, my stomach bottoming out the moment they do.

I have half a mind to say screw my other customers and beg him to take me somewhere and show me what I have so clearly been missing. It's apparent in the way every fiber of my body aches for him that I have never truly known what it means to *want* someone.

"Okay," I stutter out, feeling the blush once again flood my cheeks.

Spinning around I quickly walk away, wondering if he's purposely implying something or if I'm just interpreting things the way I want them to be.

After dropping off the checks for my last two tables, I slide inside the ladies room to wash my hands and try to get a grip on my quickly unwinding nerves.

"You don't even know him," I say to my reflection in the mirror. "Pull yourself together."

Even as I utter the words, I can't help the slow smile that spreads in front of me.

"Stop it," I warn myself.

It does me no good. He's under my skin.

I continue to try to talk myself out of encouraging this situation any further, knowing full well that if anyone is hidden behind one of the stall doors I am likely to sound like an absolute lunatic but honestly at the current moment, I'm not sure that I care much.

I stare hard at myself in the mirror, taking in my flushed complexion and the glaze over my eyes. The way my wild curls are tied up haphazardly in a knot fit perfectly with how wild and unhinged a man I don't even know has managed to make me feel.

Taking one more deep breath I finally exit the bathroom, my steps faltering the moment I catch sight of Garrett leaning against the bar speaking to Jane, the mid-day bartender. I have to do a double take, at first convinced that my mind is playing tricks on me.

Only I don't think it is.

In fact, I know it's not.

I know the moment his chocolate eyes meet mine and a wide smile crosses his clean shaved face that he really is standing just feet from me and now closing in. It's only seconds before his arms wrap around my shoulders and he's pulling me tightly against his chest.

"God it's so good to see you, Kim." He gives me another tight squeeze before releasing me, taking a step back to get a good look at me.

"Garrett?" It's all I can manage; the unexpected arrival of my ex-boyfriend placing me in a state of confusion and shock.

"What...what are you doing here?" I question.

"I missed you." He almost whines, pouting out his bottom lip slightly.

I don't know why but the action makes me cringe.

"How did you find me?" I question, having never mentioned to him exactly where I work in the handful of times we've spoken since I've been here.

He looks almost offended for a split second but then quickly recovers, his perfect exterior immediately falling back into place.

"Well I went to your dorm room first, but you weren't there. Your roommate said I could find you here." He smiles and I do my best to return the smile, at the current moment plotting my revenge on Harlee who has no idea the position she has just put me in.

I can't blame her, of course. She knows so very little about my past or Garrett. If roles were reversed, I probably would have done the same thing.

Taking a long hard look at the man in front of me, it becomes so apparently clear how much I've changed since arriving in Oregon. By the look on his face as he takes in my attire, I would say he's reaching the same conclusion.

"You look...different," he observes, gesturing to my casual clothing.

Throwing out my skirts and blouses was one of the first things I did when I arrived here. I couldn't bear to wear the clothing my parents' had forced me to endure for the last eighteen years, never being allowed to express myself through fashion.

"I feel different," I admit, flicking my eyes towards the patio where Decklan is.

My heart drops as I watch him stand, dropping cash onto the table before exiting the patio, not once looking in my direction. Disappointment creeps into my gut and quickly spreads through the rest of my body, leaving me with an almost sinking feeling.

"Kim." Garrett pulls my attention back to him.

"Sorry. I'm working," I say, shaking my head slightly.

"I know. Of course, of course you are. The bartender said you are finishing your shift up, I was hoping I could wait for you." He gives me a hopeful smile.

"Yeah, okay," I say, trying to keep my frustration in check.

I still don't understand why he would fly across the country to see someone who has made it more than clear she doesn't want to see him.

"Give me ten minutes. You can wait at the bar," I say, stepping past him to make my way back out onto the patio.

Stopping in front of Decklan's now deserted table, I pick up the hundred dollar bill he left folded on top of his check. I can't help but wonder why in hell he left so much when his bill was under twenty dollars. Do I seem desperate for money somehow? The thought makes me slightly self-conscious, but I try to push it away. I'm sure he was just being nice.

Turning to my left, I manage to catch sight of Decklan just as he climbs onto his motorcycle that is parked across the street from the restaurant. I want to go after him, find out why he left so abruptly, but the last thing I want to do is seem desperate.

I was just his waitress and nothing more. He probably sends signals like that to every female he encounters. I was foolish to let myself think he was actually interested in me. A man who oozes sex is just that. He can't help how he makes a woman feel, it's just part of who he is.

Letting out a deep sigh, I turn and make my way back inside to cash out his check and the two other tables that still remain in the indoor dining area. Less than ten minutes later, I am exiting the restaurant with Garrett at my side.

I wait until we have walked several feet away from the restaurant before turning on Garrett, causing him to stop in the middle of the sidewalk. He looks from side to side and then steps towards the wall of the building behind us.

"Why did you stop?" He seems confused.

"I can't do this, Garrett. I can't just pretend like you showing up here is a good thing. It's not. I asked you for time," I start.

"And I gave it to you." He cuts me off, keeping his voice low.

If there is one thing Garrett hates, it's public conflict. He hates drawing unwanted attention to himself.

"No, you didn't." I shake my head. "You've called me multiple times a day since

I've been here and now you just show up. I've been gone eight weeks, Garrett. Eight, and already here you are."

"Why is it such a bad thing that I miss you, that I want to speak to you, that I want to see you?" He runs a hand through his perfectly styled brown hair, clearly frustrated.

"Because I don't want to see you," I say, instant guilt swarming my stomach with the hurt that I can see in his dark eyes.

"Look." I try to soften the blow. "I told you when I left, I will never find out who I really am unless I am given a chance to figure it out. I can't be your girlfriend. I can't be my parents' daughter. I need to be Kimber. Just Kimber."

"I still don't understand why you have to rid yourself of everyone to figure out what you want in life." He crosses his arms in front of himself, his gray collared fleece bunching at his chest.

"Because everyone thinks they know what I want; what's best for me. Even you. You have spent the last three years trying to make me your perfect girl. That's not me. I'm not the daughter my parents' see me as, and I am not the kind of woman that you are going to be happy with."

"I *was* happy with you," he interjects.

"But that wasn't me. Don't you get it? That was the me I wanted you to see. The me my parents' made me feel forced to be. I don't want to be that person anymore. And you deserve to be with someone who will be honest with you and who wants the same things you want." I reach out and rest my hand on his forearm, but he flinches away from the contact.

"Who is he?" His face instantly hardens.

"What?" I ask, confused by the sudden change in his demeanor.

"The guy you're screwing; who is he?"

"I'm not screwing anyone," I say, a bit taken aback by his words.

"Yeah right, Kimber. You don't just decide to be someone else. People change other people. Someone is clearly changing you. So who is he?"

"I'm changing me," I state forcefully. "Only me. I am finally becoming the person I have always been. For the first time in my life, I'm free. I'm free from judgment, free from disappointing everyone around me, free from you and from my parents'."

"I don't understand why you can't do all of this with me?" His voice returns to the smooth proper tone he uses when he's trying to impress someone.

"Because you are not the solution, Garrett. You're part of the problem," I say, finally telling him what I should have when I ended things between us two months ago.

"So three years...three years meant nothing to you?" His anger returns.

"Of course, it did. You are a part of so many of my firsts. I will also value the time we spent together, Garrett, always. But our time together is over now. We don't want the same things in life. We're not the same people we were three years ago."

"I can't just let you go. We are meant to be together, Kim. You know it as much as I do; you're just scared."

"It's Kimber, not Kim and no, I'm not scared. I don't want to be with you, Garrett."

"I won't let you go just like that," he states, matter of fact. "I will wait as long as it takes for the girl I know is in there; the girl who loves me too."

"Well then, you're going to be waiting for a very long time because that girl is gone, and she's never coming back."

"I don't know what to do without you." He breathes, his demeanor shifting.

"You'll figure it out. I know you will," I say, pushing up on my tiptoes to lay a gentle kiss to his cheek. "Goodbye, Garrett," I say, pulling away.

I give him one last small smile before turning and walking away, leaving him standing in the middle of the sidewalk. It takes everything I have not to turn around, but at the end of the day I know I need to hold strong.

Garrett is no longer a part of my life and the clearer I make that, the better he's going to be in the end for it. There's no sense in giving him false hope, no matter how bad I feel for hurting him.

Garrett is my past.

I am my future.

What I can make of that is still yet to be seen.

# Chapter Four

### Decklan

"Well, how did it go?" Gavin looks up at me from behind the bar the moment I step inside.

"How the fuck do you think it went?" I snap, throwing my keys and sunglasses down on the bar before sliding onto one of the stools.

I throw a nod to two customers that are seated at the end of the bar drinking beer before turning back to Gavin just as he steps up directly across the bar from me.

"Whiskey?" he questions, already grabbing a glass and the bottle before I even have a chance to answer.

"Why the fuck not?" I let out a loud exhale, relaxing back into the stool.

"Why are you here anyways?" I observe, scouring the bar for signs of Jules, who typically bartends Sunday through Wednesday.

"I was bored, thought I'd give Jules the night off." He shrugs, setting the full glass of whiskey in front of me.

I'll never understand why Gavin spends his spare time working the bar. He claims it helps distract him and clear his head when things are bothering him.

"Everything cool with you?" I ask, cocking my head to the side.

"Truthfully, I just wanted a reason to avoid having to go to my aunt Lenora's birthday party. Perfect excuse." He smiles and gestures around the bar.

"What would old Lenora think if she knew you volunteered to work to avoid going to see her?" I joke.

"Considering that crazy old bat always confuses me for my numb nuts cousin, I don't think she'll notice. The cover is in case my pesky sister decides to come snooping." He snorts, turning when one of the men at the end of the bar signals for another beer.

He's right about one thing: Mia is definitely one that would double check his alibi. Being seven years older than Gavin, she has always mothered him in a way. It's only gotten worse since she's popped out two kids of her own.

Grabbing the glass in front of me, I sling back the contents in one large gulp, finding comfort in the way the liquor seers my throat on the way down. And while it somewhat takes the edge off, it does nothing to cure the deep ache in my groin left by Kimber.

All I can see is her face: those big blue eyes, the way loose strands of hair fell across her perfect skin, how fucking incredible her ass looked in those tight little skinny jeans she was wearing. I can't even start on how damn delicious she smelled.

Fuck me.

I don't know why this fucking girl is so under my skin. I know I'm going to have to fuck her. I won't be able to think straight again until I do.

"So you know the chick from last night?" I ask when Gavin reappears in front of me, moving to refill my empty glass.

"What about her?"

"She was the fucking waitress at the restaurant."

"Wait, the one you were just at?" he asks, seeming surprised by this funny little twist.

"The very one."

"So did you hit it or what?" he asks like

it's any other question.

"I told you, it's not like that. Besides, I'm fairly certain she couldn't handle me."

"When is it ever really not like that with you, Deck? You forget who you're talking to." He rolls his eyes as he pushes the refilled glass of whiskey in front of me.

"Okay, so I thought about it," I admit, grabbing the glass.

"Well then, why didn't you?" He laughs, knowing full well that when I want something, I rarely hesitate on taking it.

"Some dude showed up and was hanging on her, seemed like they were an item." I shrug, pouring my second drink into my mouth.

"Since when has that stopped you?" He lets out a laugh.

"I don't know, man. I'm all fucked up over the bullshit that happened at lunch. I guess I'm just off. Trey was really on it today." I grunt, sliding my empty glass to the edge of the bar.

"I don't know why you even agreed to go, dude. Fuck him. He's not worth your fucking time." He stops directly in front of me, his tone falling serious. "Look, dude, you've had a shit way to go. You can't fucking punish yourself forever, and you certainly can't let Trey do it for you. We got a good thing here," he says, gesturing around the bar. "Focus on that."

"Thanks," I say, Gavin reminding me
why I keep his ass around. At the end of the
day, dude's got my back like no one else.

"That's what brothers are for." He gives
me a nod, knowing he's more my brother than
Trey will ever be.

"You got shit covered here then?" I ask,
checking the clock behind the counter to see
it's just after six.

"Yeah, I'm good. Sunday and all." He
shrugs, knowing it will be a pretty slow night.

"Perfect. I'm gonna go hit the gym," I
say, pushing away from the bar.

"Have fun," he calls over his shoulder as
I push my way through the side door that
leads up to my apartment.

Climbing the stairs two at a time, I shove
the key into the lock and step inside the small
space. The moment the door closes I feel
almost claustrophobic, like the walls are
slowly closing in on me.

Yes, the gym is exactly where I need to
be. I need to release some of the fucking
tension that is built up in various parts of my
body. I need to take my aggression out on
something other than a fucking bottle of
whiskey.

I've spent too many nights staring at the
bottom of an empty bottle as is. The gym is the
only other place where I can somewhat numb

away the ache that has permanently attached itself to the pit of my stomach since the accident. When I'm there, I push my body so hard that the only pain I can feel is physical. It's one of the only ways I can find even a moment of peace.

Making my way into the open kitchen, I grab two bottles of water from the fridge before crossing into the living room-bedroom combo. It's not much, but the space is large enough for a full wrap around couch on one side and a king size bed and large dresser on the other. It's nothing spectacular, but it serves my needs perfectly.

Grabbing my already packed gym bag from the floor next to the closet, I immediately head out of the apartment through the private entrance at the back. Climbing down an outdoor set of stairs, I cross the parking lot that separates the gym from the bar.

Sliding the key into the back door of *Louie's*, a private gym primarily used for training amateur fighters, I push my way inside the moment the lock clicks. The gym is dark and silent, just how I like it. Louie never opens on Sundays, says it's his sanity day.

Luckily for me, Louie is a fan of his scotch and as such we trade off services. He drinks at my bar for free, and I have unlimited access to his gym anytime I want it, including after hours, which is usually when I come.

Flipping on the hallway light, I immediately head for the locker room to change, taking in the silence that somewhat seems to calm the chaos between my ears.

I like being alone, having access to any room and any equipment without being disturbed by other people. Working out is one of my major releases, and I can't have people fucking with me while I try to let out some aggression.

Switching on the stereo system that is wired throughout the entire gym, I settle on a rock channel, the beat of the heavy drum matching the pounding I feel coursing through my veins. After taping up my hands, I step in front of one of the large punching bags, taking a couple jabs before really getting into a rhythm. My body feels lighter with each punch I land.

This is what I need: to feel control, to feel my body physically strain and pushed to its limits. This is the only way I can let it out; the only way I know how.

**** 

"You're leaving already?" Audrey pouts out her lower lip as she watches me zip my jeans and start searching for my shoes.

"I already told you, I don't stay," I remind her, sliding on my dark blue t-shirt before finally turning back towards her.

She's sprawled across the top of the mattress, her naked body fully visible to me. I let my eyes take her in, let them rake across her petite little frame, only the sight of her doesn't even phase me; not even a little.

I've had her, and my interest is now gone. That's how it works for me. I will find a woman I want to fuck, and I fuck her. If I don't fuck her, I have trouble shaking her, hence why I haven't been able to stop thinking about Kimber since I left the restaurant three days ago. But once I land her, I know she too will lose her affect on me.

"You sure you don't want to go for another round?" Audrey pulls my attention back to the bed as I slip on my boots.

She runs her hand seductively across her milky skin, dipping between her thighs as she begins pleasuring herself in front of me. She bites her bottom lip and bends her neck backward, her long red hair fanning out around her.

She's an attractive enough girl, one I wasn't initially planning on fucking, though. I try to avoid the clingy stalker type, and Audrey has all the qualities of that type of hookup. But after the week I've had, I didn't much care who I stuck my dick in as long as it meant I could forget; even if for just a little bit.

"Stay, Deck," she moans, dipping her

fingers inside of herself.

The action does nothing for me, and I can't pretend it does. Truth be told, I barely got through fucking her the first time around, picturing Kimber's face at the end just to get myself off. If I don't fuck this girl before too long, I am likely to lose my fucking mind. I can't ever remember a time where I have denied myself a woman I want, especially going on days now.

"Sorry, I can't," I say, my words immediately halting her movements.

She pulls the sheet over herself and sits up, hitting me with hurt eyes.

"I already told you how this works," I remind her again. "Once. That's it. I didn't mislead you, so don't look at me like I did."

"I know." She pouts. "I guess I was just hoping..." She trails off.

"Hoping what?" I ask, her words making me curious.

"That I could be the one." She blushes slightly as she finally meets my gaze. "You know, the one you would be willing to break your one-time rule for."

"What are you talking about?" Her question catches me a bit off-guard.

"I just thought... I don't know. I really like you, Decklan. Like *really* like you." She seems embarrassed by her confession.

I don't know when this little infatuation

started for her, but I guess I should have seen the signs. She's been coming to the bar more and more frequently, wearing skimpier outfits each time clearly trying to snag my attention.

Standing, I let out a loud exhale.

"There's a reason I only sleep with a woman once. And that's because I don't ever want to mislead a woman into believing I can give her more... I can't." I lean forward and kiss the top of Audrey's head.

"You were incredible," I reassure her, slipping on my leather jacket before quickly exiting her bedroom.

Sliding on my helmet the moment I reach my bike parked on the side of the road, I throw my leg over the sleek black exterior and fire the engine to life. Seconds later I'm speeding down the street, weaving through parked cars that take up a good portion of the neighborhood roadways.

I drive towards the bar, but once I get close I decide to just keep going. It has to be getting close to midnight at this point, and the wind whipping around me becomes colder with each moment that passes. But I just keep driving.

I need to clear my fucking head.

I need to *not* go home where I will likely numb myself with shots of whiskey and maybe even fuck another woman. The same pattern and yet the results it yields are always the same. It's an endless cycle and one that brings me very little comfort anymore.

Veering onto the freeway, I increase my speed, taking advantage of the sparse late night traffic. I drive so long that by the time I finally pull off at the Springfield exit, my legs and hands are damn near numb from the drop in temperature.

I don't know what I'm doing here. My hometown is a place I avoid like the plague, but for some reason, it's the place I feel like I need to be tonight.

Following the familiar roads I spent my entire youth traveling, it takes only a few minutes before I'm pulling my bike off into a vacant old parking lot that sits directly across from the Springfield cemetery.

Killing the engine, I climb off and deposit my helmet onto the seat before pulling a cigarette out of my jacket pocket. Lighting it, I take a deep inhale before setting off across the street.

The cemetery is closed, of course, the main gate locked and inaccessible to vehicles. But that doesn't stop me. Clenching my cigarette between my lips, I climb up the eight feet iron fencing that surrounds the entire graveyard, hopping to the ground the moment I reach the top.

Straightening my jacket, I set off into the darkness, knowing exactly where I am heading. I weave in and out of various headstones, heading towards the back row that sits several hundred feet from the entrance.

When I finally reach my destination, I drop my cigarette, stomping out the cherry with the heel of my boot before taking the final remaining steps towards the large dark headstone in front of me.

*Conner Roderick Taylor*
*January, 3 1994-November 29, 2008*

My eyes scan the tombstone for several long seconds, trying to remember his face, his voice; all the things that I feel are slipping away with time.

"Hey, little brother," I finally manage to say, swallowing down the hard knot in my throat as I reach out and rest my hand on the cold stone.

# Chapter Five

## Kimber

"Honestly, honey, I don't know why you don't just come home. You don't belong in Oregon. You belong here, with your family and people who love you." My mother drones on in my ear as I cross campus, heading to *Lovett's* directly from my English Lit class, only half paying attention to what she's actually saying.

"We've been through this. I'm here to stay, at least until I complete my degree. After that, well, I guess I'll just have to figure it out as I go," I say, readjusting my bag that hangs heavily on my shoulder.

"That is no plan at all," she interjects,

still not able to support my decisions simply because they are mine and not hers.

"I'm not doing this again, Mother. I've gotta get to work. Talk soon, okay," I say, ignoring her attempt to keep me on the phone as I hit the end call button and slide the device into the front pocket of my jacket.

Of course, I avoid telling her that I'm off work for the next two days and actually just heading over to pick up my paycheck. Cutting her off with an excuse is the only way I can end a conversation with her on a relatively good note.

I hate that it has to be this way. I hate that I can't share in the joys of my college experience with my own mother. Unfortunately, she's too controlling to back down, and I am too far gone to cave to the ridiculous demands that I drop my classes and return home to attend the school of their choosing with no say at all over my future.

It takes less than fifteen minutes before I am pushing my way inside the front door of *Lovett's*, giving Johnson, the older gentleman who mans the bar in the evening, a nod and small smile before dropping my heavy bag next to the bar and sliding into a vacant stool.

"Need your paycheck?" Johnson asks the moment he approaches me, sliding a glass of water across the bar.

"Please." I smile, taking a long drink of

the cold liquid.

"Here you are, dear." He returns just seconds later, setting a white sealed envelope in front of me.

I glance up to thank him but immediately freeze when I catch sight of the man who has dominated my thoughts for the past few days, sitting just cattycorner across the bar from me, a glass of golden liquor in front of him.

*Decklan.*

He meets my gaze almost instantly, causing my stomach to twist and the ground beneath me to shift slightly. What is he doing here?

"Did you have class today?" I hear Johnson's words, but it takes me several moments to process them enough to form an answer.

"Um...yes, just finished my last class of the day." I break away from Decklan's stare to turn my attention back to the gray-haired man in front of me. "Have you been this slow all evening?" I attempt to distract myself from the gray eyes I can still feel burning holes in the side of my face.

"Pretty much." He shrugs, turning his attention to the front door when two middle-aged men walk in and take a seat on the other side of the bar. "Well, I guess I'll see you next week then." He nods before setting off in the direction of the new arrivals.

Before I have time to even process Decklan being here, he appears at my side, pulling the stool out directly to my left before taking a seat.

"Funny seeing you here." His lips turn up in a one-sided smile while his eyes remain focused forward.

I try not to stare too long at his profile, at the curve of his jaw or the long scar that starts at his temple and then disappears into his thick mess of dark blond hair.

"I work here," I manage to get out though my voice doesn't quite portray the sarcasm that I intend for it to.

"But you're not working tonight?" he asks, spinning his stool towards me, prompting me to turn my head inward to face him.

"I'm not," I confirm, my heart feeling like it might actually beat through my chest at any moment.

"Let's get out of here." His request throws me off guard a bit, and I suck in a shaky inhale.

"And go where?"

"Anywhere you want to go." He shrugs. "Are you hungry?"

"I could eat," I answer, even though my appetite checked out of the building about three minutes ago when my eyes landed on the incredible looking man now sitting next to me.

"There's this amazing little pizza place about ten minutes from here. You in?" He gives me the sexiest grin I have ever seen, and I all but melt right on the spot.

"Um. Well... I..." I stutter out, not sure if I should. I mean, I don't even know this man.

"I promise I don't bite." His smile widens as he leans forward, closing the distance between us to just mere inches. "I mean, unless you're into that sort of thing," he whispers, his eyes holding mine completely captive.

I can feel the heat rush my face, the crimson color fill my cheeks as his words wash over me. It slowly spreads through my limbs, warming every inch of my body.

"Well?" he questions, tilting my chin upwards with his hand, not allowing me to break the contact.

"Okay," I breathe out my reply on a shaky exhale.

"Leave your bag, we'll come back for it," he says, grabbing it from the floor as he stands. "Would you keep this here for, Kimber?" he asks Jefferson who passes by us at that exact moment.

"Of course." Jefferson nods and retrieves my bag from Decklan, stuffing it underneath the bar for safe keeping. Without another word he nods and walks away, busying himself with another group of customers who have just entered the bar area of the restaurant.

"Ready?" Decklan holds his hand out to me, watching me intently as I take it and allow him to guide me off of the bar stool.

Tucking his hand around my fingers, he leads me out of the bar, not stopping until we reach his motorcycle which is parked across the street. My feet falter the moment we approach the sleek black bike.

"Let me guess, you've never been on a motorcycle before?" he asks, releasing my hand to retrieve the helmet resting on the seat of the bike.

"Never," I breathe, my insides twisting violently.

His smile only widens as he deposits the large black helmet on top of my head.

Everything in me is telling me to run. I shouldn't be doing this. I shouldn't be leaving with a man I don't know who could end up taking me God knows where, let alone getting on the back of his motorcycle.

But something about the way he looks at me silences that voice, reassuring me that I can trust him. But can I really?

"Should you be driving?" I stutter out, embarrassed to even ask the question. "I mean, you were just drinking," I add on.

*Wow, way not to sound like a total loser, Kimber. Smooth. Real smooth.*

Decklan runs a hand through his messy hair, pushing the fallen strands away from his eyes as he settles onto his bike; hitting me with an amused smile.

"I only had one, and I promise you, I would never put you on this bike with me if I was in any way inebriated. I may drink and drive, but I don't drive drunk." His tone falls serious, and for a moment I almost feel bad for even asking the question.

"Aren't you going to wear a helmet?" I can't control the word vomit that continues to spew from my mouth, feeling my embarrassment grow with each moment that passes.

*Shut up, Kimber. Shut up and get on the bike.*

"I only have one." He taps lightly against the visor of the helmet on my head, halting my movements when I reach to remove it. "You're wearing it." His tone is absolute. "Trust me, you are much more valuable than I am." He winks, reaching for my hand.

I hesitate for a brief moment before I finally lay my hand in his. Stepping where he tells me to step, I fling my leg over the bike as I settle onto the seat behind him. Reaching around, he grabs my wrists securing both of my arms around his waist.

"Whatever you do, do not let go," He instructs, firing the bike to life.

The vibration beneath me is enough to cause my breath to catch in my throat and sends my heart beating even more violently against my ribcage, fear coursing through my entire body.

I take a shaky inhale as I secure my grip, my hand skirting across his hard abs through his open jacket and thin black t-shirt as I do. Trying to ignore the sudden surge of electricity I feel being secured so tightly against him, I lay my head against his back and clench my eyes closed tightly; praying to God this isn't the biggest mistake of my life.

I feel the weight of the bike shift as Decklan takes off and proceeds to weave through traffic. He handles the motorcycle with such ease that my nerves settle slightly after a couple of minutes. Even still I'm not brave enough to open my eyes for any of it.

By the time the bike slows and the vibration beneath me dies off, I feel like I am stuck in my current position from holding my body so rigid for so long. Decklan senses this and lets out a deep laugh, his back vibrating slightly against my chest.

"It wasn't that bad was it?" he asks when I still make no attempt to move.

"I don't think I can move," I admit, not sure if I can't or simply don't want to.

"Here." He unlocks my hands from his waist and slides off the bike, careful not to move me as he does.

Once his feet hit the ground, he turns, reaching up to unlatch the helmet and pull it off of my head before depositing it directly in front of me on the seat.

"There." He smiles, pushing my wild tangled mess of hair away from my face. "Better?"

He reaches for me when I nod, lifting me under the armpits as he slides me from the back of his motorcycle and sets me gently to the ground just inches from him. Reaching out, he pushes my hair behind my shoulders before tipping my face upwards so that my gaze meets his.

"Glad I can say I was your first." He gives me a wicked smile, laughing when he sees the blush once again take over my face. "Your first motorcycle ride." He laughs again, clearly finding amusement in the fact that my brain doesn't seem to function properly around him.

"Come on." He takes my hand once again, causing me to spin around as he leads me through the parking lot.

I don't recognize where we are, but it's a pretty populated place; a long strip mall of businesses and small little restaurants. It doesn't take me long to locate the pizza place I assume we are heading towards. There's a large window that makes up the front of the store, *Pops Pizza* painted brightly across the glass.

I quicken my steps to keep up with Decklan's long strides given he's quite a bit taller than me. I would say he's at least six feet where as I stand just around five four.

He slows to a stop just short of the entrance to the pizza place, leaning forward to open the front door before ushering me inside, his hand falling to the small of my back as he does. The contact causes a shiver to run down my spine and while Decklan doesn't say anything, I know without a doubt he notices.

Avoiding his gaze, I allow him to lead me through the establishment, my eyes taking in the small pizza parlor.

It's a pretty standard size; a square dining room that has four booths along the far wall, two of which are occupied by other customers, and two square tables in the middle. There's a long counter that runs along the front wall and is open to the kitchen where I briefly catch sight of a younger looking man rolling out dough.

Decklan doesn't stop until we reach the booth that sits in the far corner of the room. Removing my jacket, I hang it on a wooden hook that's attached to the post of the booth before sliding into the seat. I can't keep my eyes off of Decklan as he removes his own jacket, the thin material of his black t-shirt clinging to his clearly muscular body in all the right ways.

I flick my eyes to Decklan's face as he slides into the booth across from me, his slow spreading smile telling me he knows exactly what I was looking at.

"So this place is pretty good?" I ask, taking a menu that is wedged between the wall and the napkin holder, desperate for a distraction.

"The best." He smiles, watching me intently.

"So what do you recommend?" I ask, laying my menu face up on the table in front of me.

"You can't make a wrong choice here. But I have a weakness for the thin crust pizza with pepperoni." He settles back into the seat, crossing his arms in front of his broad chest.

"Sounds good to me," I say, closing the menu. "So..." I let out a small sigh of relief when we are interrupted by an older lady who immediately approaches our table.

Her black pants and matching button down shirt are covered in flour, her salt and pepper hair tied back in a frizzy bun. I can't help but notice the way her face lights up when her eyes land on the man across from me. At first, I think maybe she just realizes how attractive he is. I mean I'm sure older women are no more immune to his charms than younger ones are, but then I realize that's not it. The recognition in her eyes tells me she knows him.

"Decklan Taylor as I live and breathe." She hits Decklan with a wide smile.

"Ms. Marie." He stands, giving her a one-armed hug. "How are you? How's Bob?" he asks, sliding back down into the booth.

"Oh, you know that old fart, still kicking." She laughs. "He's at home with the grandkids tonight. But he'll sure be disappointed he missed you." She gives him a warm smile. "What's it been, two years?"

"Probably close to that. I don't get down this way that often," he explains.

"And Gavin, how is that trouble maker?"

"Same as ever." He smiles warmly back at the older woman.

"Why does that not surprise me?" She shakes her head before seeming to finally realize that someone else is sitting at the table with Decklan.

"And who is this beautiful creature?" She gives me a toothy grin, waiting for Decklan to introduce us.

"Ms. Marie, this is Kimber, a friend of mine."

"So nice to meet you." I smile up at the older woman, reaching out to shake her hand when she extends it to me.

"You too, my dear. Any friend of Decklan's is a friend of mine. Spent half my days trying to keep this heathen out of trouble I did."

"Is that so?" I smile, flicking my eyes to Decklan who gives me a playful shrug.

"Story for another time I suppose." Marie laughs. "Now, what can I get for you? The usual?" She turns back to Decklan.

"That sounds amazing," he confirms.

"And to drink?"

He surprises me by saying water, and I indicate that I will take the same. In the three times I have been in this man's presence I've never seen him drink anything but alcohol. It's good to know he's chosen water, especially considering he is my way back to campus.

"Coming right up." Marie smiles, spinning as she makes her way behind the counter.

"Old friend of yours?" I smile, gesturing towards where the older woman was just standing.

"I grew up just a couple of blocks from here. I practically lived here every day after school. Marie and her husband Bob were like second parents to me and Gavin."

"Gavin. He's a friend of yours?" I question.

"More like my brother," he confirms.

"You've met him already," he says, explaining when I hit him with a look of confusion. "At *Deviants.*"

"The bartender?"

"Yes, he was bartending the night you were there but he's more than that; we run the bar together. He's my business partner." He nods towards Marie who reappears with our waters.

"Should be out shortly," she says, sliding the glasses in front of each of us.

"Thank you," I say, smiling in her direction as she turns and walks away. "Wait, so you own the bar?" I jump right back into our conversation the moment she's out of earshot.

"I do. Well, with Gavin. We bought it four years ago. Of course, it was a complete dump back then, but we managed to turn it around."

"I would say so," I agree, having seen the bar firsthand.

Even though it's a bit out of my comfort zone, my statement is the absolute truth. *Deviants*, while wild and a bit untamed, is a very nice establishment.

"You didn't seem too thrilled with it last Saturday." A slow smile creeps across his impossibly handsome face.

"It's just... a little different than what I'm used to," I admit.

"I'm starting to gather there are a lot of things that are different than what you're used to." He leans towards me, his elbows coming to a rest on top of the table in front of him.

"Is it that obvious?" I question.

"It's not a bad thing." He reaches out and takes my left hand, twisting his fingers around mine. "In fact, I find it quite refreshing." His voice drops low, and my stomach immediately erupts in butterflies.

"So you said you're from around here?" I redirect, desperate to take the conversation off of me.

"I am," he confirms not giving me anything else.

"Why did you leave?" I ask when he makes no attempt to continue.

"Why did you?" His obvious avoidance of the topic tells me everything I need to know.

"It's a long story." I sigh, my eyes falling to our hands as his thumbs trace circles across the back of my skin.

"Lucky for you I've got all night." He grins, the action causing my stomach to bottom out.

Every little thing this man does makes me feel like I am going to melt into a puddle at his feet. He just makes me feel, I don't know, alive I guess. There's no other way to explain it. The world just suddenly seems so much more vibrant.

"I..." I start but then stop, pulling my hand away from Decklan as Marie reappears at our table, sliding a large pizza and two plates between us.

While the food looks incredible, I'm not sure my stomach will accept it. It's so knotted and full of nerves it's almost painful. Taking a deep breath and letting it out slowly, I try to push aside the nervous energy surging through me.

I wait for Decklan to grab a slice of pizza before I help myself to one as well. I make sure he isn't watching me as I slowly lift the slice to my lips and take a small bite. He's right of course, the pizza is amazing, but it still takes everything I have to force it down.

I can't focus, can't find a way to silence the loud thud in my ears as my heart pounds rapidly in my chest. I can't concentrate on anything except the way his incredible gray eyes keep finding mine, the heat behind his intense stare, and how my entire body tingles beneath it.

*I am in so much trouble...*

# Chapter Six

## Decklan

This is fucking torture.

Having Kimber wrapped around me, clinging onto me for dear life as if I'm the only thing tethering her to the world; it's enough to make me fucking insane. All I want is to bury myself deep inside of her and shatter her perfect little exterior. With her pressed so tightly against me, it's nearly impossible not to pull over somewhere and do just that.

She tenses as I maneuver the bike around a curve in the road, her grip growing impossibly tight. I can't help but let out a light laugh, the sound lost to the noise of the wind whipping around us.

Pulling up outside the dorm building Kimber advised me that she lives in, I pull into a vacant parking spot and kill the engine. She immediately loosens her grip; the loss of her arms wrapped around me the last thing I want to feel right now.

Fuck this girl has me so mixed up.

She slides off the back of the bike before I make any attempt to move, handing me the helmet as she steps around beside me.

"Thank you for dinner." She gives me a sweet smile, the familiar blush returning to her pale cheeks. "And for the ride." She pushes up on her tiptoes and leans in, laying a light kiss to my cheek.

When she lingers there a second too long, I can't fight the urge to taste her any longer. Turning my face inward, I latch my fingers into the back of her hair and pull her mouth roughly to mine.

She tenses for a brief moment, my action clearly catching her off guard, before she finally relaxes into the kiss, her lips parting slightly on a soft moan as I trail my tongue lightly across her lower lip.

Her hand finds my upper thigh, her nails digging into my flesh as I deepen the kiss, pulling her towards me. I let out a deep groan as I slide my tongue against hers, feeling her tremble slightly against me. It's enough to make me almost frantic with *need*.

But just as I feel like I might split apart if I don't have her right now, she slowly eases out of the kiss, her breath coming in short spurts as she pulls away and meets my gaze with heated eyes.

"I... I should go." She pants, stumbling backward slightly as she steps out of my embrace.

I open my mouth to speak but then close it again, not really sure what to say. Instead, I sit silently on my motorcycle under the dark night sky and watch her disappear from view.

Letting out a slow shaky exhale, I run my hands through my hair. What the fuck was that? I can't ever remember a time when a kiss has gotten me so worked up.

I must want this girl a lot more than even I realized.

****

"Wait, so let me get this straight. You took her out to dinner?" Gavin stares at me in disbelief from his bar stool. "Like a date?"

"Why is that so surprising?" I ask, not seeing the big deal.

"Because *date* is not part of your vocabulary, dude. I don't think you've ever taken someone on a date."

"It was just pizza at Maria and Bob's place." I shrug, taking a swig of my beer before setting it back down onto the counter.

The bar closed over an hour ago, but neither Gavin nor myself seems to be in any rush to call it a night.

"Still, dude, that's huge for you." He leans over the bar and drops his empty bottle into the trashcan.

"It's really not that big of a deal. She's not the kind of girl you just fuck. She's the kind of girl you get to know first." I drain the rest of my beer, sliding my empty bottle towards Gavin who immediately drops it into the trashcan as well.

"That may be, but I've never known you to waste your time on girls that require any type of work to bag." He lets out a gruff laugh.

"I don't know, man, I'm just sick of the same old shit I guess. Women who are willing to spread their legs for anyone are a dime a dozen. Women like Kimber, now that's a prize."

"Whatever does it for you I guess." He shrugs. "She got any hot friends that aren't quite so difficult to woo into bed?" He raises his eyebrows suggestively.

"Maybe. Her friends that came here with her last weekend seem to fall under the work-free category from what I gathered." I let out a slow exhale, stretching my arms.

"Then what are we waiting for?" He laughs.

"I'm not lining up girls for you to fuck. You can take care of that shit yourself." I open a fresh beer and toss the bottle cap at his face, laughing when it pings off the top of his forehead and then bounces to the floor.

"Not cool, dude." He shakes his head before pushing out of the chair to his feet. "Alright, I'm over your pansy bullshit. I'm heading out." He grabs his jacket off of the back of the bar stool, sliding it on.

"Be careful," I say, knocking his fist with mine when he holds it out to me.

"Always am." He throws on his cocky ass smile before practically skipping towards the exit. "Don't forget to lock this shit," he says, pushing the front door open; disappearing outside without another word.

The door no more than latches closed before I feel the onset of what has become almost a daily struggle in my life. Headaches so severe they are downright disorienting. I drop my head into my hands, the sudden and violent pain shooting through my skull causing the entire room to seem to shift sideways. I groan out, squeezing my forehead with my hand as I wait for the pain to pass. It always does, eventually.

Just another reminder of how much the accident changed. How much it changed me, both physically and emotionally. I guess that's what happens when you suffer severe head trauma; it fucks you up in all kinds of ways.

While the headaches are enough to bring me to my knees sometimes, they have nothing on the pain I feel festering deep within myself. I can take the physical pain, no matter how bad it gets. I think of it as somewhat of a punishment; God's way of torturing me even further for what I've done.

Another sharp pain and my stomach twists violently, my body fighting to deal with the intensity of it. I struggle to take a deep breath, and it seems I can't get my lungs full enough as the pain continues to grow.

"Fuuuuck," I scream out, pushing against the bar as I try to fight through the feeling that my head is on the verge of exploding.

I try to focus on my breathing, forcing my lungs to inhale and exhale despite the fact that it feels like there is a thousand pounds sitting directly on top of my chest. But just when I feel like I can't take any more and my body has reached its capacity for the pain coursing through it, it eases, dying away completely within a matter of seconds.

Straightening my posture, I slowly open my eyes one at a time, afraid to push too hard too fast and have the pain come billowing back. Taking another deep breath, I push out of the bar stool, my body still feeling slightly shaky.

As soon as I'm sure it has passed, I make a grab for the bottle of whiskey directly across the bar from me. Not wasting my time on a glass, I tip the bottle to my lips and let the heated liquid drain down my throat.

When I finally resurface, a third of the bottle is gone and my chest burns like fire. I relish in the pain, the heat searing my insides as it soothes my mind.

Sliding on my jacket, I make my way towards the front door, pulling out a cigarette and lighting it the moment I step out into the chilly night air. Taking a deep drag, the smoke fills my lungs, calming me.

It always takes me a few minutes to come out of the daze my pain-riddled episodes leave me in, and tonight is no exception. Taking another hit from my cigarette, I try to focus on the taste, the smell, the way the nicotine seems to calm the small tremor still running through my hands.

****

"So are you gonna take me somewhere private or what?" The sexy redhead in front of me leans over the bar and trails her hand down the side of my face.

"That depends." I pull away from her touch.

"On what?" She slides back down into her stool.

"On whether or not you can make it until close without puking," I say, already knowing she won't make it another hour before she finds her head in a toilet.

"Done." She smiles, taking the shot in front of her before spinning around and rejoining her friends on the dance floor.

"What is that, five now?" Val steps up next to me, an amused expression lighting up her face.

"Six, but who's counting." I let a laugh roll through me.

"I swear to God, women have no shame." She laughs, nudging me in the side with her elbow.

"You would know." I slide two shots across the bar to one dude before nodding to the next guy who immediately asks for a beer.

"That's why I like them so much." She runs a hand through her boy short dark hair and gives me a playful smile. "One of these days you're going to have to let me show you how to *really* please a woman." She laughs when I arch my brow at her.

"I think I got that covered," I reply, lining the bar with four shot glasses before pouring each one full of vanilla vodka.

"Well, the offer stands regardless." She hits me with a teasing grin before sliding down the bar to help another customer.

Val was the very first bartender we hired after the bar opened. She's a bit of a spit fire but given the atmosphere, it seems to work in her favor. I never have to worry about her being able to take care of herself with this rowdy crowd. She's small, but she definitely knows how to fend for herself.

I can't help but shake my head at her when she leans across the bar and lays a kiss directly on the mouth of one of our male customers. Despite the fact the she's one hundred percent same sex interested, she still plays her role nicely. She's here to make money, and she knows how to do just that.

Turning my attention back to the endless amount of drink orders, I quickly fall back into a groove, sliding drinks across the bar without even really paying attention as to who I'm serving them to. As long as they have a yellow wristband that says they are over twenty-one, I don't need to know who they are.

We are slammed tonight. So much so that I had to pull my ass out of the bed I've been laying in all day to come down and help Val and Gavin bartend. Of course, had Matt not called off they would have been fine without me. That fucker better actually be sick. If I find out he called off on a Friday night for some other bullshit reason, his ass will be looking for a new job.

"Can I have a water please?" I hear a familiar voice and look up to find a big set of beautiful blue eyes staring back at me.

*Kimber.*

It takes me a moment to get over my shock of seeing her here, but I quickly recover.

"What are you doing here?" I smile, grabbing a glass, quickly filling it with water before setting it on the bar in front of her.

"I'm celebrating." She shrugs, taking a long drink of water, her gaze temporarily leaving mine.

She looks incredible tonight. Her petite frame is draped in a royal blue sleeveless dress that clings to her chest and flares at her waist. Her blonde hair is pinned back loosely, a few escaped strands falling around her face. Like the other times I've seen her, her makeup is light and natural, not that she even needs it. I don't know that I have ever met anyone as naturally beautiful as the woman standing in front of me.

Just watching her full lips close around the rim of her glass is enough to make my groin tighten. Fuck...

"What are you celebrating?" I wait until she lowers the glass before asking.

"My birthday. Angel and Harlee wouldn't let me out of going out. I figured if they were going to force me to celebrate, I might as well use it to my advantage." She points to the dance floor where I immediately spot her two friends from last weekend.

"They don't waste much time," I

observe, watching the two girls who have already managed to draw quite a crowd of men around them. Shaking my head, I turn my attention back to her.

"No kidding." She laughs, looking back towards me.

When her eyes meet mine again, an instant blush floods her face. It's deep enough that it's visible even under the dim bar lighting. Fuck, it takes everything I have not to reach across the bar and touch her.

I can still taste her, feel the way her bottom lip trembled against mine. My eyes immediately find her mouth, and I suck in a ragged breath. That kiss is all I have thought about since last night.

"Happy Birthday," I manage to get out, trying to pull my shit together as I once again meet her gaze.

"Thank you." She gives me a shy smile, clearly still not sure if she made the right choice coming here.

I want to tell her she didn't. In fact, coming here was the worst decision she could have made. There is no way I am going to be able to let her walk out of here tonight. I can't fight how deeply I crave this girl. But then again, something tells me she already knows this, and that is exactly why she is here.

"How about a birthday shot?" I ask, grabbing a shaker glass.

"Oh no, thanks." She shakes her head. "I don't drink."

"Ever?" I ask, surprised by her response.

"I mean, I have before but I don't usually. Besides, I'm only nineteen, and I don't want to get you in trouble." The color of her cheeks only deepens.

Fuck me; this girl is going to be the fucking death of me.

"Nineteen..." I let it hang it there for a long moment. I knew she was young but fuck, I didn't know she was *that* young.

"How old are you?" She hits me with curious eyes.

"Twenty-five." I give her a short answer before changing the subject back to the matter at hand. "Now how about that birthday drink? I insist." I hit her with a reassuring smile when she opens her mouth to protest, snapping it shut when she finally accepts that I'm not going to take no for an answer.

Proceeding to fill the shaker glass with ice before adding a variation of liquids to it, I can feel her eyes on me as I pour the purple drink into her glass and slide it towards her.

"Purple Hooter." I laugh lightly at how apprehensive she looks. "It's good, I promise; very fruity."

"How do I know I can trust you?" She narrows her eyes at me.

Leaning across the bar, I stop only when

my face is just a few short inches from hers.

"You can't," I speak low, my gaze holding hers.

I'm close enough that I can hear her sharp inhale and see the way the heat floods her eyes. It's the first time I've ever been convinced that her mind is exactly where mine is.

Without another word she slowly lifts the glass to her lips, her eyes not leaving mine as she pours the liquid down her throat.

# Chapter Seven

## **<u>Kimber</u>**

I know he's watching me. I can feel his eyes burning into the flesh of my back as I move freely across the dance floor, my blue A-line dress swirling around me. Harlee and Angel finally managed to drag me out here after four shots of the purple liquid Decklan has kept on endless supply for all three of us over the last hour.

Every time we go to the bar there's another set of shots lined up. After the first shot Decklan made me, he gave me three yellow bracelets and told me to have fun. I feel guilty for taking advantage of him in this way; I can only imagine the trouble he could get into if someone found out that not one of us is actually old enough to drink.

Even still, I can't deny how good it feels to finally just let loose. I came here to shed the girl I was in West Virginia; to reinvent myself. Since I've been here, I have done very little in the way of that. I guess it's harder to branch away than I realized it would be.

"Shot, shot, shot, shot, shot." I hear Angel chant beside me before I feel her arm loop through mine and begin to pull me from the dance floor.

"You really don't need me do you?" I object, not ready to stop dancing yet; my body high on the warm buzz running through my veins.

"Considering it's your birthday." Harlee appears at my other side. "Yes, we do."

We finally manage to fight our way through the crowd and reach the bar, but to my disappointment it is Gavin, the sexy bartender/co-owner I met last weekend, who serves us and not Decklan. Of course, the other two seem quite pleased by this fact, considering they know Decklan is off limits.

Not like I have some claim on him or anything. But having heard me go on and on about him all day today, I think they pretty much gathered that I am *very* interested. Not to mention that is why they insisted on coming here tonight. They had to meet the man that had me all sorts of flustered and babbling like an idiot after the kiss he laid on me last night.

My hand instinctively goes to my mouth, my fingers tracing lightly across my bottom lip as I remember the feeling of his touch, his taste, how powerfully he commanded my entire body.

Snapping out of my daze, I try to act unfazed by Decklan's absence. Taking one of the six shots Gavin sits in front of us, I tilt it to my lips, pouring the sweet liquid down my throat.

Setting the empty glass back on the bar, I catch sight of Decklan just as he appears from a door to the right of the bar with a spunky little red head fast on his heels.

My stomach twists violently and an instant rage swarms my body. I don't have to think very hard about what they were doing behind wherever that door leads. I can tell by the girl's disheveled hair and the way Decklan adjusts his shirt.

It's only seconds before his eyes meet mine, and I know instantly that my face must give away my reaction to what I just witnessed. I can tell by his own reaction, the way his features seem to tighten. Ripping my eyes away, I grab another shot and pour it down, then another, ignoring the cheers of my two friends who are clearly enjoying watching the uptight good girl from West Virginia pound shots like a mad woman.

"Let's go," I holler over the music, not waiting for the girls to join me as I push my way back through the crowd.

I don't stop until I have reached the center of the dance floor, the effects of the shots starting to take hold as the music pounds through my ears. Within seconds, I feel two arms slide around me. Turning my face slightly, I'm met with a waft of cologne and the cocky smile of a good looking twenty-something.

I have no idea who the guy is, but I don't have it in me to protest when he tightens his grip on me and starts grinding against my backside. Normally I would be appalled by the action but tonight, tonight nothing is off limits. I'm sick of being Kimber Lynn James, the sweet, privileged girl from Wales, West Virginia. Tonight I'm just Kimber.

Lifting my arms in the air, I let the thumping music take control, allowing my body to sway and move with the rhythm. I don't care when the man's hands travel across my abdomen. I don't protest when I feel his hands thread through my hair as he pulls my head back. I barely register his lips on my neck when he leans forward and sucks on the sensitive flesh just below my ear. Hell, I don't even open my eyes until I feel the loss of him completely.

Jumping slightly, I turn just in time to catch sight of Decklan's face before his hand closes around my forearm, and he forcefully pulls me from the dance floor. I try to object, ask him what the hell he's doing, but my voice is lost to the noise around us.

Leading me towards the bar, he doesn't loosen his grip on me until he's pushing me inside of the same door I just saw him exit a few moments earlier with the red head. I stumble slightly the moment we're inside, looking around to find myself standing in a small stairwell.

"What the fuck do you think you're doing?" Decklan's voice is rough as he steps towards me, guiding me backward until my back becomes flush with the wall behind me.

"Having a good time," I answer sarcastically, not able to hide the hurt in my voice.

"You sure? Because it looked to me like you were trying to send a message." He presses his body into mine, pinning me between him and the wall.

"Why would I do that?" I look up to find his face hovering just inches from mine.

"You tell me."

"Is this where you bring all your girlfriends?" I break eye contact as I lift my hands to his chest and push, surprised when he takes a couple of steps backward.

"I don't have girlfriends." He runs a hand through his messy hair.

"Oh, I'm sorry. Is this where you bring all your sluts?" I regret it the moment I say it, but the liquor flowing through me makes it difficult to control my tongue.

"Why don't you just say what this is about?" he challenges, his nostrils flaring slightly. "You saw me coming out of here with another woman, and you immediately assumed the worst," he states.

"Do you blame me?" I question, gesturing to him.

"No," he states simply. "Had I wanted to fuck her, I would have."

"Had you wanted to?" I stumble out, finally meeting his gaze again.

"I live here." He points up the stairs. "I came up to grab a clean shirt after having a drink spilled on me. When I came down, she was waiting for me. I told her to go home."

"So you didn't?" I break off, feeling all sorts of jealous girlfriend crazy right now and one hundred percent aware how desperate it makes me look.

"No. I didn't touch her." He takes a step towards me, stopping when his body is once again directly in front of mine. "How could I when all I can think about is touching you?" His words are just above a whisper, but they sound so loudly through my ears they echo several times before the statement finally registers.

"Then do it," I challenge, struggling to keep my breathing even as I meet his deep gray gaze.

He hesitates for only a moment before his lips crash down onto mine, his tongue seeking entrance into my mouth within seconds. I grant it, moaning when his taste and scent invade all of my senses.

My hands find the back of his neck as I pull him closer to me, my fingers digging lightly into his flesh as the *want* coursing through my body starts to take hold. I feel like I can't get him close enough. I want to feel him everywhere.

*Everywhere.*

I barely register my feet leaving the floor until I feel Decklan's body shift below mine as he begins climbing the stairs, his arms securing me tightly against his muscular frame as he continues upward.

He pushes his way through another door, but at this point, I am far too preoccupied to look around. The only thing that matters is this: the way his body flexes as he lowers my feet to the floor, the way his hands skirt up my bare back as he pulls the fabric of my dress over my head leaving me in nothing but my white lace panties.

My eyes adjust to the darkness enough that I can see his silhouette in the light from the street lamp that filters into the otherwise dark room. I can see the ripple of his muscles as he drops his shirt to the floor, hear the rapid intakes of breath he takes as he pushes me back onto the bed and slowly removes my last article of clothing.

My entire body goes ridged as he spreads my legs open, allowing his eyes to trail across my now bare exterior. I fight to keep my hands at my sides, my instinct to cover myself becoming almost unbearable as I feel the heat of his gaze take me in.

I hear the buckle of Decklan's jeans and the rustle of fabric as they fall to the floor, the anticipation of what's to come making every part of my body ache with the need for his touch. The rip of a condom wrapper comes next, Decklan settling between my legs just moments later.

He pushes my hair from my face, his lips once again finding mine as he kisses me deeply. I jump slightly when I feel his hand slide between us and settle between my legs. When I feel his fingers push inside of me, all coherent thought seems to leave my body.

I become greedy, lifting my hips to meet his hand as he pumps his fingers inside of me. I can feel the effect his touch has on me, the pleasure causing my body to pool around his hand.

"Please," I whimper when he abruptly
pulls his hand away, leaving me unsatisfied
and wanting so much more.

"Please what?" His mouth settles over
mine again as he gently pulls my bottom lip
into his mouth. "Tell me what you want,
Kimber," he demands, grinding his rock hard
erection between my legs.

"You," I whimper again. "I want you."
My words are pleading, begging even.

I've never had a man's touch control me
the way his does. I can feel each flicker of
movement across every surface of my body.
Decklan has shown me more pleasure in the
matter of a few short moments than Garrett
did during the entire three-year span of our
relationship.

"Please," I grind out again when he
slides just the tip of his erection inside of me
and stops there, his face hovering just inches
above mine.

"Is this what you want?" he asks,
pushing forward another inch.

"Yes," I hiss, digging my nails into his
shoulders, trying to move him deeper inside of
me.

"This?" He continues to tease me,
moving so slowly I can't control my mounting
frustration.

"Oh my God just fuck me already," I

practically growl, realizing instantly that this is exactly what he'd been waiting for.

He immediately plunges inside of me, both of us crying out from the intensity of our bodies coming together. Pulling back, he slams into me again, pulling yet another scream of pleasure from my mouth.

I try to hold it back, the moans and whimpers that seem to keep flowing from my mouth, but I can't. He's pulling everything from me, making me feel every ounce of pleasure as he thrusts harder and harder inside of me.

It takes minutes— or maybe it's only seconds— before a warm incredible sensation starts to work its way through my lower belly. The feeling is so foreign and yet my body seems to recognize it just the same. Decklan senses my heightening desperation and pushes my legs further open, pounding into me so deeply I swear I feel him everywhere.

"Decklan," I cry, my body so overcome with pleasure I'm not sure how to control myself.

I cling to him for dear life, his mouth finding mine as he swallows my cries of pleasure; the earth seeming to literally fall out from beneath me. My body explodes around him, and I swear I have never felt anything like it before in my life.

It comes in waves, washing over me,

warming every single inch of my body until I can feel the effects to the very tips of my fingers and toes. Decklan makes me feel every ounce of it as he continues to thrust inside of me, milking every bit of pleasure from me that he can before finally finding his own release.

He lets out a deep groan, pumping inside of me several more times before finally slowly to a stop. Relaxing down on top of me, his lips find my cheek first, then my forehead, followed by the tip of my nose before he finally presses them gently against my own.

I can feel myself pulse around him as he sweetly kisses my mouth, his tongue sliding against mine as his hand pushes the tangled mess of waves that have escaped my hair tie away from my face.

"That was..." I start to say, not quite sure I have the words for it. "Unlike anything I've ever experienced," I admit, struggling to catch my breath. "I've never...you know." I break off, a bit embarrassed over my clear inexperience.

"You've never what?" He pulls back slightly, his face hovering above mine.

"I've never had a..." I break off again, covering my face with my hands.

"You've never had an orgasm before?" He pushes my hands away and forces me to look at him.

I shake my head, feeling the heat flood my face as he looks down at me. He studies me for a long moment, his face showing his clear confusion over my statement before it shifts more to a look of determination.

He slowly pulls out, causing me to protest the loss of him almost immediately. Once again relaxing his body on top of mine, he lets out a light laugh and shakes his head.

"Oh don't worry. We're just getting started." He breathes against my lips, sucking the bottom one gently into his mouth. "I haven't even begun to show you the things I can do to this sweet little body," he whispers, sealing the promise with a deep kiss.

# Chapter Eight

## **Decklan**

I have never met such a perfect fucking contradiction. So sweet and innocent and yet Kimber has allowed me to see a side of herself I doubt anyone else has seen; a wild untamed side that I never expected.

She's not at all what I had her pegged as.

Reaching out, I push a few stray strands of hair away from her face, unable to keep myself from smiling when she crinkles her nose and shifts slightly.

I have no idea what time it is. All I know is that I can't sleep. I can't close my eyes long enough to even come close. I'm too busy watching Kimber. I can't get past how beautiful she looks laying here in my bed, her hair sprawled out on the pillow behind her as she sleeps peacefully on her stomach, her face turned towards me.

Just the sight of her stirs something deep inside of me, something I thought I would never experience. She makes me feel *something* other than the pain.

For the longest time, I have wandered through life trying to numb it with alcohol and random women. I'm having a hard time processing that just watching her sleep brings me a peace that neither of those things has ever given me.

It's terrifying and yet so fucking liberating at the same time.

It's not lost on me that not only is she the first girl I have ever allowed to stay the night, but she's also the only girl I have slept with more than once. *Ever...*

I don't know why.

I don't know what it is about her that makes me feel so different.

The thought plagues me over and over again as I watch her back rise and fall with each breath she takes. I count them; each inhale, each exhale, until they all fucking blend together into nothingness.

**\*\*\*\***

I wake abruptly, my eyes shooting open as I take in the drab ceiling above me. No nightmares... I can't remember the last time I slept through the night without having at least one.

Turning my face to the side, the sight of Kimber lying next to me is enough to send a galloping panic through my chest. I've never woken up next a woman before, and to say the experience is unsettling is a bit of an understatement.

Remembering that I abandoned Val and Gavin last night, I decide I should probably run downstairs and make sure the place is still in one piece. I know this is my excuse for escaping my current situation, and I'm okay with that. I just need a minute to sort through this.

Pushing back the covers, I roll out of bed, careful not to wake Kimber who is still in the same position on her stomach as she was when I finally dozed off last night.

She shifts when the bed creaks, rolling to her back but remains asleep. I can tell by how peaceful she looks: her expression soft, like an angel.

*An angel who just crawled into bed with the fucking devil.*

Quietly crossing the room, I retrieve my pants and shirt from last night off of the floor, sliding them on before slipping on my shoes and heading out the door, downstairs to the bar.

Pushing my way inside, I jump slightly when I see a bright eyed Gavin sitting at the bar drinking a cup of coffee from the bakery across the street. I can tell where it's from by the flowering fucking design that swirls across the lavender to-go cup.

Looking around, I notice immediately that the bar has already been cleaned; the bar stools turned upside down on the tables to allow the freshly mopped floor to dry. Shay must have been in and out early this morning.

"Mornin." Gavin offers me a knowing smile and nods.

"What the hell are you doing here this early?" I ask, crossing behind the bar to retrieve the cash from last night, something I do every morning.

"Well, it's not really all that early." He laughs, prompting me to glance at the clock to see that it's already afternoon.

Holy shit.

I can't remember the last time I slept this late. Sleep is usually not a friend of mine. Then again, that's certainly not the only thing that is different this morning.

"And I've already dropped the deposit." He adds when I open the cash register to find the money already gone.

"What the hell has gotten into you?" I

turn curious eyes on him, knowing how out of character this type of behavior is for Gavin.

"Just felt like helping out a friend." He takes a large drink of his coffee, avoiding my gaze.

"Fuck that. You forget I fucking know you, dude. What the hell is up?" I pin curious eyes on him.

"Nothing." He shakes his head. "I just wanted you to be able to take it easy this morning. You know, considering that you bounced out on me and Val two hours early, and you were still going at it well after the bar closed last night. You really should get a new place, or at least learn to keep your girls quiet." He smiles mischievously and lifts the coffee cup back to his mouth.

"How was she?" He tacks on after taking a long drink.

"I'm not doing this with you." I cross my arms in front of my chest and lean against the back counter behind the bar.

"Since when?" He seems a bit surprised. "We always share war stories. You can't hold out on me now. Unless..." His smile spreads. "She's still here isn't she?"

"What if she is?" I try to keep my tone casual.

The last thing I want to do is have Gavin make this a big deal when it's not.

"Shut the fuck up." He slaps the bar in

surprise.

"Dude." I point at the ceiling, gesturing to upstairs. "Can you keep it the fuck down?"

"My bad." He laughs. "So you're really not gonna tell me anything?" He pushes again.

"Nope." I shake my head slowly.

"That good huh?" His smile is so big at this point I swear his face is going to split apart.

"Better." I drop my head back on a laugh when he jumps up from his stool.

"I knew it. I fucking knew that hot little piece would be stellar in bed. Fuck. I should have made my move first." His words cause anger to boil slightly in my chest.

I don't know why. It's not like we haven't had similar conversations. But this is different. I don't want anyone talking about Kimber like she's just another piece of ass. Then again, do I really expect her to be anything but exactly that?

"Well too bad for you, you didn't." I shrug, trying to swallow down my statement as the reality of my situation starts to really take hold.

So what if I let her stay the night? I've been craving her for so long I needed a few times to really get her out of my system. That doesn't mean anything. It doesn't mean that I am somehow changed and that everything will be different.

I'm still me and if there's one thing I know about myself, it's that even if I wanted to give Kimber more I couldn't. I'm not capable of being the type of man she needs; the type of man she deserves.

Gavin opens his mouth like he is about to say more but then snaps it shut when the door leading from my apartment opens and Kimber emerges, her hair now pulled back into a loose knot and her face free of makeup.

She looks absolutely breathtaking.

"Well, good morning," Gavin speaks, pulling her attention towards him as he slides back down onto his bar stool.

Her cheeks immediately go pink, and she stutters for a moment before finally managing to get her words out.

"Good morning." She looks towards me, her blush deepening as she nods in my direction and steps up to the side of the bar.

"I'm Gavin, but you can just call me Gavin." He leans forward, close enough that he is able to extend a hand to her. She reaches out and shakes it gently, clearly not sure what she's gotten herself into by coming down here.

"Kimber," she replies sweetly, pulling her hand away after a brief moment.

"Did you happen to see my purse by any chance?" She looks at me, unable to hide how uncomfortable she feels in this situation.

I have to remind myself it's a situation

she has never found herself in before. I still can't believe she's only been with one man, now two, and that the other man was someone she dated for three years. Three years and she had never had even one orgasm with him. Fuck, I'm tempted to look the fucker up and give him some fucking pointers.

"It's by the register." Gavin points behind me, cutting into my thoughts. "I found it on the stairs this morning." He shrugs, not the least bit apologetic that he clearly was snooping.

Something tells me he knew Kimber was here the whole time but was simply waiting to see if I would admit that I let her sleep over, considering it's not something I have ever done before.

I turn, retrieving the small black bag before crossing towards her, laying it on the bar the moment I reach her. She looks up, meets my eyes for only a fraction of a second before turning her attention to the bag.

"Thank you," she responds, digging inside before pulling out her phone. "Shoot." She looks flustered and slightly panicked.

"What is it?" I ask, pulling her gaze back towards me.

"I was hoping Harlee would have text me. I completely bailed on them last night." Her voice is riddled with guilt. "I have no idea how or if they got home."

"Taxi took them both home just after one thirty," Gavin speaks up, relief instantly flooding Kimber's face. "I put them inside of it myself."

"Thank you." Kimber meets his gaze.

"It's what we do." He shrugs like it's no big deal, but I can tell there's more to it.

Deciding not to push the topic in front of Kimber, I keep my thoughts to myself but make a mental note to ask him about it later. Gavin doesn't personally take care of anyone. The fact that he called a cab and even walked the girls out tells me he was trying to score brownie points. I'm just not sure with whom yet.

"I can't believe they just left me like that." She shakes her head, her cheeks heating crimson when she realizes she made the statement aloud.

"Don't worry. I let them know you were preoccupied. I think they were more than happy to leave you behind." He raises his eyebrows playfully at her which seems to only deepen her embarrassment.

"Well, I should probably get going." Kimber's hesitant gaze comes back to mine.

"I'll take you home," I say, ignoring Gavin's surprised expression.

What does he expect me to do, have her pay a cab for over an hour trip when I can just as easily give her a lift? Then again, I guess even something that considerate is a bit out of character for me.

"Oh, you don't have to do that." She slides her phone back into her purse before pulling out a set of keys. "Angel's car is out back. I'm sure she expects me to bring it home."

"Okay." I nod, unable to ignore the disappointment that seems to settle over me.

*Fuck.*

*Get your shit together, Deck.*

"Well, at least let me walk you out," I say as I step out from behind the bar.

"Okay," she gets out weakly, turning towards Gavin. "It was nice to officially meet you." She gives him a small wave before allowing me to lead her out of the back door and into the nearly vacant parking lot.

I squint into the bright sun, locating what I can only assume is Angel's car, a small red Prius, sitting at the back of the lot all by itself. I follow Kimber towards the vehicle, not really sure what the fuck to say.

Since when do I have trouble figuring out what to say to a woman?

I stop directly next to Kimber once we reach the car. She turns inward to face me, clearly not sure what she should say either.

"Have you ever been to a Ducks game?" she finally blurts after several long moments of tense silence. "As in the college football team?" she tacks on.

"I know who the Ducks are," I remind her, having grown up just minutes from the University of Oregon.

"Right." She shakes her head. "Well, they are playing a big game against some rival school next Saturday. I don't know much about football," she explains. "But Harlee said it's a lot of fun. We're meeting some people early in the day to tailgate, and then we're gonna catch the game. We have a couple extra tickets if you'd like come with us." She scrunches her forehead in the cutest fucking way. "I mean, you don't have to of course." She rambles. "But I've never tailgated before, and I think it could be fun. But you're probably busy. You know what, forget I asked." She turns, ripping open the car door.

"Do you always do that?" I laugh, pulling her attention back towards me.

"Do what?" she questions.

"Invite someone and then un-invite them." I can't fight my amused smile.

"No, of course, you can come if you want," she stumbles out.

"I'm just giving you a hard time." I reach out, unable to resist the urge to trail my fingers along her jawline.

The contact causes her to take a shaky inhale making it nearly impossible for me to rip my gaze away from her eyes which seem to flood with desire.

"But I appreciate the invite," I tack on, fighting the urge to lean in and kiss her.

"Of course." The blush of her cheeks only deepens. "Maybe we can do something else sometime?"

"Maybe." I try to shake off the fog that seems to have settled over me, finally letting my hand drop away.

"Okay." She nods, wearing the disappointment on her face plain as day. "Bye, Decklan," she gets out weakly, sliding into the driver's seat.

Something about hearing her say goodbye causes dread to fill the pit of my stomach. How can I be so sure and yet so unsure about something at the same time? A part of me wants to grab her, carry her ass back upstairs and never let her leave again. The other part of me, the rational part, knows I'm doing the right thing by letting her leave.

She immediately closes the door of the car and fires the engine to life. Throwing me a weak smile and a small wave, she quickly pulls out of the parking lot, forcing me to stand here and watch her drive away knowing full well it will likely be the last time I ever see her.

A girl like Kimber doesn't belong in my world. She's too sweet, too innocent. I would ruin her. She's too fucking special to be ruined by the likes of me. I have proven time and

time again that I am incapable of not hurting
the ones who get close to me. I can't hurt her
like that. I'd never forgive myself, and I
already carry around too much fucking guilt as
it is.

# Chapter Nine

## Kimber

Stepping inside my dorm room, my stomach flutters knowing I'm about to face my two friends after what happened last night. I let out a slow exhale when the dimness of the room settles over me, the curtains drawn, and a light snore filling the air.

I quietly close the door and slip off my shoes, thankful that I have a little more time to process last night's events. Or at least, that's my initial thought until I hear a throat clear lightly, and I spin to see Harlee sitting on top of her bed, her hair tied into a knot on top of her head, legs crossed in front of her, her trusty Kindle resting in her lap.

Looking back towards my bed, only now do I see the black hair sprawled across my pillow, realizing that it's Angel sleeping and not Harlee.

"Good morning." Harlee flips her Kindle over on the bed and pins her gaze on me.

"Morning," I whisper, crossing the room towards her, flopping down on the edge of her mattress the moment I reach it.

Lying back across the foot of the bed I let out a deep sigh, not sure if I want to laugh, cry, or apologize profusely for the choices I made last night.

"So...how was it?" Harlee keeps her attention focused on me.

Turning my head towards her, I can't help the splitting grin that takes over my face the moment my eyes meet hers.

"Words can't even begin to describe it," I answer truthfully, surprised by how good it feels to just say this fact out loud. "I'm sorry I disappeared on you."

"Are you kidding?" She swipes her hand through the air. "I would have done the same thing to you." Her smile widens.

"What's that say about us as friends?" I laugh, dropping my arm over my forehead.

"It says we're damn good ones because we want each other to have fun." She nudges me with her foot as she straightens out her legs on the bed. "Besides, I wouldn't have left if I didn't feel comfortable leaving you where you were."

I don't know that I would have left her regardless, considering you never really know people these days, but I don't push the issue. I have to remind myself that in Harlee's world something like this is completely acceptable.

"Don't let her lie to you, she would have left you either way." Angel's voice causes me to jump slightly.

Pushing up on my elbows, there's enough light filtering into the room that I can see her sitting up in my bed, her dark hair seeming to stick up in every direction.

"Screw you, whore." Harlee laughs, throwing a pillow in Angel's direction. It falls short and lands on the floor a good foot from the bed.

"You better have brought Sally back in one piece." She hits me with stern eyes as she refers to her car.

"Not a scratch on her." I sit up, tossing the keys still clutched in my hand at her.

She snags them out of the air, laughing when they nearly connect with her forehead.

"Now—" Angel pins her eyes directly on me, "—tell us everything. I want every last detail. And don't you dare think about leaving anything out."

****

"So are you a big football fan?" Travis, one of Angel's friends asks, sliding down next to me on the tailgate of the pickup truck I'm sitting on, turning a sweet smile in my direction.

"Not really," I admit, forcing down another drink of the beer in my hand.

It's not the first time I've had beer, but I swear it's worse than the last time I tried it. Even still, I continue to drink it, determined to make myself like it even if it tastes like animal pee.

"No?" he questions, pointing to the *Ducks* hat and hooded sweatshirt I am currently wearing.

"Harlee—" I explain, "—She wanted me to fit in." I straighten the bill of the hat before adjusting my ponytail through the back.

"Well, you wear it well." His smile deepens, his blue eyes fixed on mine.

He's a good looking guy, one that I have met one time before today. If I remember correctly, he used to date Angel which you would never guess by watching them together. They seem more like brother and sister than people who would date each other. Even still, it's not hard to see what Angel saw in him.

He's at least six-two, broad shoulders, very athletic looking, but it's his smile that's the real kicker. It's one of those brilliant dimpled smiles that make even the most uninterested girls do a double take.

"Thank you." I finally acknowledge his statement, turning my head to look out over the twenty or so people that have gathered in our area to tailgate before the big game.

It's only four in the afternoon but most of our group is already drunk, having started drinking before noon. And while I have nursed a couple of beers as to not be the odd woman out, I have taken them down slowly enough that I feel completely sober.

"So you're from the east coast right?" Travis pulls my attention back to him, sliding off his hat as he scratches his forehead.

"West Virginia." I nod.

"I've never been out that way. Is it much different?" he asks, clearly just trying to find a reason to talk to me.

Normally I'd be flattered, maybe even interested, but unfortunately given the events of this week, his feeble attempt to connect with me annoys me more than anything.

"Completely." I give him a short answer before throwing a small wave at Angel who is leaning into the side of the truck next to us watching me intently.

She raises her eyebrows up and down and throws me a wicked smile before turning and crossing the space to where a large group of people are playing a game of corn hole.

I can't help but roll my eyes. I know

what she's up to and it's not gonna work. I'm
not like her, I can't just sleep with someone
and then turn around and forget all about
them. I'm not programmed that way.

I wish I could say the same for Decklan
who clearly *is* programmed that way. I also
wish I could say that I saw this coming; the
blow off that follows a one-night stand, but I
wasn't even a little prepared. I think that's the
worst part; thinking that there's more to it
than just sex only to find out there's not.

"Did you hear me?" I jump slightly,
realizing Travis is once again talking.

"Sorry. What?" I shake off the fog
surrounding me and turn to find him studying
me curiously.

"I asked if you were hungry." He smiles.
"They have some amazing hamburgers over
there." He points to a food tent set up just a
few yards from us.

"No, I'm good, thanks." I take another
long drink of my beer that despite the cool
temperatures have gotten warm over the last
hour that I've been drinking it.

"You sure you don't want to walk over
with me; might warm you up to move a little."
He adds when a small shiver runs through me.

"I'll be fine." I force a smile, not missing
the irritation that briefly crosses his
handsome face as he stands and pushes away
from the truck.

\*\*\*\*

I want to enjoy myself, I really do. I want to feel the excitement that swarms over the crowd as the Ducks continue to dominate their opponent, but I just can't get into it. I thought getting out would help get my mind off Decklan, but it's actually only made it worse.

Of course, it doesn't help that Travis made a point to sit in the seat directly next to me or that he's spent the first half of the game hitting on me; the amount of alcohol in his system clearly giving him a false confidence on his chances of landing me.

It makes me angry that I can't enjoy the attention he's giving me and even angrier that all I can do is compare him more and more to Decklan with every moment that passes. To say he doesn't stack up is the understatement of the year. Truth is, he doesn't even come close which in turn only causes my frustration to mount.

Is this what I signed up for? To be used and in turn ruined for any future man that may come into my life? I just don't get it. I don't get how he can just disappear after the night we spent together.

I tried calling the bar once, having never gotten his phone number, but I was given the run around by the female who answered and decided not to call again. It's bad enough that I can't stop thinking about him; I don't need the rest of the world to see how pathetic I am, too.

Lifting the beer bottle to my lips, I drain the remaining contents as the crowd around me once again erupts in triumph. I have no idea what's happened nor do I care. As desperate as I am to get the full college experience and really put myself out there, I am more desperate to see Decklan.

I don't know what I expected from him. I guess that just goes to show that no matter the connection you feel to a person, it doesn't change who they are at their core.

Even still, I can't let it lie. I can't just walk away without knowing if it was something I did. I have to see him. I won't be able to think straight until I do. Maybe it's the beer, or maybe I am just sick of sitting back and letting life pass me by. But right now there is only one place I want to be, and it's not here.

Pushing out of my seat, I hear Travis say something as I turn, but I ignore him. I slide through the row of seats until I reach the edge where Harlee is sitting, squeezed between two frat guys, looking like she is on cloud nine.

"I'm gonna head out," I yell over the roar of the crowd.

"What? Why?" She hits me with a

confused expression.

"You stay," I say when she attempts to stand. "I have a something I need to take care of. I'll see you back at the dorm later." I lean in and give her a brief hug and a reassuring smile before sliding past her into the aisle.

Taking the stairs two at a time, by the time I reach the floor level platform I am gasping for air. The drop in temperature over the course of the evening makes it difficult to get a good deep breath, the cold stinging my tired lungs.

Reaching the parking lot within a few minutes, the cab I called is already waiting for me by the time I reach the street. Sliding into the back seat, I ramble off my destination and settle in, knowing it's going to be a long ride to Portland.

****

The cab finally slows to a stop outside of *Deviants* just after ten-thirty. It's clear to see from the crowd of people standing outside smoking that the place is hopping though I would expect nothing less on a Saturday night.

Handing the driver some cash, I quickly exit the cab, forgetting completely about my attire until a drunken girl leaning against the building makes a comment under her breath loud enough that I can hear it. For a moment,

I have the urge to turn around and punch her right in the face, but I shake the anger away, not really sure where it's stemming from.

After showing my identification to the man at the door, I finally push my way inside, my ears immediately assaulted by the pounding noise of the live band playing on stage. I didn't even know they had bands play here though I guess it shouldn't come as a surprise.

Fighting my way through the thick crowd, I stop at the edge of the bar. I don't recognize either of the bartenders working, and I can't seem to locate Decklan anywhere. Momentarily turning my attention to the stage, I watch as the singer jumps around like a lunatic as he sings some rock/pop hit that I recognize but can't pinpoint.

Turning my attention back to the crowd, I let out a relieved sigh when I spot Gavin lounging on a barstool smack dab in the center of a group of girls. Shaking my head, I quickly make my way towards him, having to literally push two girls out of my way in order to reach him.

His face tightens the moment he recognizes who I am but it's brief and quickly replaced by a drunken smile.

"Kimber," he hollers over the noise.

"Where is he?" I don't waste my time with pleasantries.

"Who?" He plays stupid but gives me a knowing smile.

"You know who." I don't indulge his playfulness, the hour and a half car ride making me more than a little irritable and my nervousness over being here shutting out my ability to care if I seem rude.

"He's in the gym." His tone drops. "Backdoor, across the parking lot." He gestures towards the back of the room.

Nodding, I immediately head in that direction, pushing my way outside and crossing the crowded parking lot before I even once even consider my actions. I'm too blinded by my determination to really see things clearly though I more than recognize how out of character this is for me.

Grabbing the handle I can only assume leads into the gym, I pull open the heavy steel door and step inside, immediately knocked back by the volume of the rock music pounding from a surround sound system. The hallway I am standing in seems to act as a tunnel, only magnifying the sound.

Taking a deep breath, I force my feet to move, my eyes scanning a large room the moment I enter it. This place reminds me of an old boxing gym from the Rocky movies, more of a warehouse than a stereotypical gym. Various equipment runs along the far right wall, a boxing ring directly in the center, with punching bags to my left.

My stomach twists when my eyes finally find him...

Decklan.

He's in the far corner of the room laying waste to the punching bag in front of him. His back is turned towards me so he doesn't see me as I take hesitant steps in his direction. I don't stop until I am just a few feet from him. I'm far enough that he doesn't sense my presence but close enough that I can see the tiny droplets of sweat that trickle down his bare back as he lands punch after punch to the bag in front of him.

I'm mesmerized by the way his back muscles flex and move with each jab he takes. It's quite possibly the sexiest thing I have ever seen, and I have to force myself to hold my composure and not melt right here on the spot.

I watch him for several long moments, wondering what he's thinking, wishing I could run my hand along the dampness of his back and feel the heat of his flesh beneath my palm. The thought leaves me biting down on my lower lip just to control the urge.

Gently clearing my throat, the moment the noise registers around him, he freezes, his hand still in the air mid-swing. Turning slightly, the moment his eyes catch mine my stomach bottoms out.

He looks so incredible it takes everything I have not to physically tremble at the sight of him. His chest and ab muscles are glistening, the light hitting the beads of sweat in a way that gives his skin an almost glowing effect. His hair is damp and disheveled, hanging haphazardly in front of his eyes. And while all of this is enough to bring me to my knees, nothing could have prepared me for the look on his face when my eyes finally find his; so full of anger, but more so full of pain. Regret floods through me at the sight.

I open my mouth to speak but immediately close it again. I should never have come here. I don't know how I let myself make such a rash decision. I'm a stupid, stupid girl.

The long moment of silence seems to stretch endlessly between us. Decklan's eyes not once leaving mine as he holds my gaze, his pained stare clearly conflicted.

# Chapter Ten

## **Decklan**

I told myself I wouldn't do this. I promised myself. But looking at her standing there, so completely fucking adorable in her oversized sweatshirt and hat, I can't stop myself. I have to have her.

Without a word I close in, pushing her roughly into the wall behind her before tilting her face up towards mine. Tossing her hat to the side, her hair pools around her shoulders as I close my mouth down on hers. She gasps at the contact but quickly responds, her body seeming to come alive under my touch.

It's been the longest fucking week and even the most attractive of women haven't been able to keep my interest enough for me to find any sort of release from the frustration and pain that seems to play on constant repeat.

But it only takes one touch with Kimber, one tremble of her bottom lip as I suck it into my mouth, one soft moan as I grind myself against her, and everything seems to disappear. I lose myself in her touch, in the way her body seems to take me to another place entirely.

Lifting her up without breaking away from her lips, I carry her into the locker room, not stopping until I reach my bag sitting on the edge of the bench that lines the center of the room. Setting her to her feet, I drop my face into her hair and inhale her sweet scent, a low growl escaping my throat as my need becomes animalistic and almost too much to bear.

Fumbling in the side pocket of my bag, I finally locate a condom. The moment I have it in my hand I spin, pinning her against the steel row of lockers, smiling when she gasps as the cold metal brushes against the small of her back where her sweatshirt has ridden up.

I rip open her jeans, shoving them roughly down, so desperate to feel myself inside of her that not for one second do I give a fuck about anything but just that. She stumbles slightly, getting off one shoe and then the other before kicking her pants to the side, her hands finding my bare sweat-riddled chest.

She trails her hand down my abdomen, her heated eyes holding my gaze as her fingers dip lower. I let her reach just centimeters from where my erection is at the ready, but I don't let her touch me. Grabbing both of her hands, I pin her arms above her head with one hand while I push my gym shorts down my hips and slide the condom on with the other.

I just need to feel her.

It's the only thought I have.

*I need her.*

Dropping my mouth back to hers, I lift her from the ground, rocking back to secure her legs around my hips before thrusting inside of her so violently a small cry of surprise floods from her lips. Pinning her roughly against the locker once more, I drop my face into the crook of her neck as I begin pounding inside of her.

I know I'm being rough, probably too rough really, but she only spurs me on further, urging me to go deeper, fuck her harder. It sends me spiraling out of control. It's been too long, and I find my release sneaking in within a few short moments.

I don't want it to be over. I want to bury myself as deeply as I can inside of her and never come out, but I can't stop my need for release from taking me under. It builds so deeply inside of me that when I feel her clench tightly around me, I explode, not able to hold it in any longer.

I continue to move, the feeling of her quaking around my hard cock so incredible I think I could almost go again right here on the spot. Slowing my thrusts, I make sure I have drained every bit of her orgasm from her before finally sliding out and gently lowering her to her feet.

Having trouble catching my breath, I drop my forehead against hers; regret immediately starting to creep its way in.

"I'm sorry," I whisper.

"Don't be." She pulls back slightly and hits me with gentle eyes.

"What are you doing here?" I fumble out, my mind still not fully processing that she's really here.

How is it that just when I feel myself reaching that breaking point, the one I have teetered on for years, she shows up, allowing me to find solace in her body.

"I needed to see you." Her soft voice is enough to gut me with guilt.

"You shouldn't have come," I say, stepping back as I adjust my gym shorts.

"Why?" She seems hurt by the statement, reaching down to retrieve her jeans from the floor before sliding them on.

"I can't give you what you want, Kimber," I say, stepping back to let her pass me.

She sinks down onto the bench and looks up to meet my stare, her crisp blue eyes burning into mine. *Those damn blue eyes that seem to see through me so clearly.*

"How could you possibly know what I want?" She cocks her head to the side.

"I guess I don't," I admit, not sure how else to respond.

"Then don't assume. I barely know you. It's not like I'm going to turn around and start picking out my wedding dress." Her tone is even and free of emotion.

"Fair enough." I can't fight the smile pulling at the corners of my mouth.

This girl is a fucking enigma.

I just can't quite seem to figure her out. At first, she seems quiet and timid like she's afraid to let herself be seen. But the more time I spend with her, the more I'm realizing that there is so much more to her than that. Little by little I see the real Kimber, the tough untamed girl she keeps tucked away, shining through.

"Then I'll ask, what is it that you want?" My smile only widens when she crunches her forehead like she's really thinking about it.

"Well for starters, what does a girl have to do to get some food around here?" She hits me with a playful smile, completely eliminating the mounting tension with one statement.

I can't control the laugh that escapes my lips at her comment. One minute I think I know exactly where this is going, the next she throws me for a complete loop. It's refreshing to not know what to expect.

"I might know a place or two." I grab my bag from the bench, throwing it over my shoulder. "But first, I need a shower." I extend my hand to her which she willingly takes, allowing me to pull her to her feet.

****

"Good?" I laugh, watching Kimber eat the pancakes in front of her like she can't seem to get them into her stomach fast enough.

I guess she worked up quite an appetite after our shower, her still damp hair evidence of how she let me take her against the tiled walls. Just the thought of her cries of pleasure and the sound of water and skin hitting skin makes my groin tighten.

"Oh my God, so good." She laughs after swallowing down a large bite. "I feel like I haven't eaten in days."

"I told you this place has the best pancakes." I relax back into the booth seat as I take a long drink of my water, trying to redirect my line of thought.

"You weren't kidding." She lets out a deep exhale and pushes her plate away. "But I can't possibly eat another bite." She drops her napkin to the side after wiping it gently across her mouth, the action making me want to lean forward and taste the sweet reminisce of syrup left behind on her lips.

Tearing my eyes away from her mouth, I look up just in time to see the waitress returning with our check. Without even giving her the opportunity to set it into the table, I hand her a couple twenties and advise her to keep the change. The middle-aged brunette gives me a warm smile and then backs away with a nod, allowing me to turn my attention back to Kimber.

"You didn't need to pay for me," she interjects, her eyes darting towards the waitress who is already several feet away before turning back to face me.

"Isn't that what a gentleman does?" I smirk when she narrows her eyes on me.

"There are a lot of words I could use to describe you, Decklan, but gentleman isn't one of them." She laughs when I fake offense.

"Ouch." I hold my hand to my chest, just over my heart.

"Shut up." She shakes her head, the cutest fucking giggle making its way out of her throat as she pulls her phone from her pocket and checks the time. "I probably should be getting back. Harlee is probably wondering where I am." She slides from the booth, waiting for me to follow her action before pushing to her feet.

"I'll drive you home," I offer, the thought of her having to take a cab this late at night all the way home not something that sits well with me.

"And freeze to death on the back of your motorcycle? No, thank you." She shakes her head as she pushes her way outside, snuggling deeper into her sweatshirt the moment the cool night air settles down over us.

"Then stay with me." The request leaves my lips before I can stop it and catches us both off guard.

Even though I desperately want to take back the invitation, I also can't deny how the thought of her bare again, withering in pleasure beneath me, sounds too fucking good to pass up; even if it is completely against my better judgment.

"It's really not necessary. I don't mind taking a cab." She gives me a sweet smile.

I want to insist, force her to come back with me, but even I know having her stay the night is probably the last thing I should do. I already fear my actions are sending the wrong message but fuck me, I just can't help myself.

This girl fucks with my head.

"Not gonna happen." I shake my head. "Come on, I can use Gavin's truck to take you home."

"Are you sure, Decklan? You really don't have to." She hesitates, clearly fearful that she's putting me out.

Truth be told, I'm just not ready to let go of her yet.

"I know. I want to." I hold my hand out to her, tangling my fingers around her small palm as I lead her the two blocks back towards the bar.

"Can I ask you a question?" I can feel her eyes on the side of my face as we stop just shy of the front entrance of *Deviants*.

"Depends on the question." I spin to face her.

"Why didn't you try to get in contact with me after last weekend?" She has trouble meeting my gaze as she mutters the question. "I mean, did I do something?" Her eyes finally find mine.

"It has nothing to do with you." I can't resist the urge to reach out and brush a strand of hair away from her face. "I guess I can't really give you an explanation." I shrug, not really sure what to say to her. "Other than I'm an asshole."

"I don't buy that." She holds my gaze, her expression challenging. "I think there's a lot more to you than you let people see." She turns, pulling open the front door of the bar and stepping inside before I have time to even process her statement, let alone respond.

I follow Kimber as she weaves through the crowd of people towards the bar, spotting Gavin lounging on a stool with a few other people just moments before Kimber stops in front of him.

"Guess you found him." Gavin gives Kimber a wide smile before turning hesitant eyes in my direction.

I give him a tight nod, not sure if I want to thank him or punch him for telling Kimber where she could find me. On one hand, tonight has been exactly what I needed. On the other, I fear that it has only made this situation more complicated, and I don't do complicated.

"Give me your keys." I hold out my hand, not bothering to actually ask.

"What the fuck for?" he slurs, clearly having spent a good portion of his night on the receiving end of the bar.

"I'm gonna drive Kimber home." I keep my hand extended.

I make no attempt to move until he finally rolls his eyes, reaches into his pocket, and drops the keys into my palm.

"Crash upstairs tonight. I don't want your ass sleeping on the floor again." I give him a stern look before turning back to Kimber who seems to be watching our interaction curiously.

"Come on." I grab her hand, immediately leading her through the bar and out of the back exit.

The moment we step outside I pull a cigarette out of my jacket and press it between my lips. I catch Kimber's gaze just as I light it, turning my face towards her as I take a deep drag.

I half expect her expression to be one of judgment but am surprised to see it's more so a look of curiosity.

"What?" I ask, turning my face to let the smoke billow from my lungs.

"Nothing." She shakes her head, dropping my hand when I stop directly next to Gavin's black pickup truck. "Just trying to figure something out."

"What's that?" I ask, taking another deep inhale.

"You," she answers simply.

"Well, good luck with that." I let out a gruff laugh as I blow upwards, trying not to get smoke in her face. I may be an asshole, but I'm not that inconsiderate. "Come on." I peel open the driver's side door and gesture for her to climb across.

I take two more deep drags off my cigarette before stomping it out with the heel of my boot. Climbing into the cab of the truck, I turn my face towards Kimber whose eyes are still firmly focused on me.

"Keep looking at me like that and we won't make it out of this parking lot," I warn, her mouth dropping open slightly at my statement as she takes a sharp inhale.

"Maybe that's the point." She teases, snapping her seatbelt, her gaze remaining focused directly on me.

# Chapter Eleven

## Kimber

The ride back to campus is a silent one. There is this mounting need to say something, yet neither of us seems to be in any rush to break the silence or say what needs to be said. The further we drive, the more I feel Decklan withdraw.

It's clear he has walls put up. He's so hesitant to just *be*, which tells me he's not used to giving up any amount of the control or restraints he places on himself. I wish I could figure it out but he's extremely hard to read.

I can't help the disappointment that settles over me when he finally pulls into a spot outside of my dorm building, throwing the truck into park.

"Thank you for the ride." I unsnap my seatbelt before turning my gaze on Decklan.

He's gripping the steering wheel tightly, his eyes focused directly in front of him. Not really sure what to do, I sit for several long seconds before finally deciding I should just go. Reaching for the door handle I push it open, the cool night air flooding into the cab of the truck as I slide out.

"Night, Decklan," I say as casually as possible, giving him a small smile when he finally turns his dark eyes in my direction.

"Goodnight, Kimber." He gives me a stiff nod before turning his attention forward again.

Frustrated by how quickly things seem to shift between us, I slam the door the shut with a little more force than I intend before setting off in the direction of my building. I can feel the tears welling behind my eyes before I even reach the sidewalk just a few short feet away.

I know it's foolish. I know crying over a man like Decklan is useless and will get me nowhere, but I can't lose the disappointment I feel. Shaking my head, I manage to push the tears away before a single one has the chance to fall. If there's one thing I have mastered, it's keeping my real feelings hidden. Taking a deep inhale, I climb the small stone stairwell that leads to the front door of my dorm building.

Pulling my key from my pocket, I no more than slide it into the lock when Decklan's voice washes over me from behind, halting my movements.

"Kimber, wait."

Pulling the key back, I turn to see him jogging towards me, stopping just feet from the bottom step.

"I'm sorry. I don't know how to do this." His words come out labored through his rapid breathing.

"You don't have to do anything, Decklan. I get it," I say, shrugging. "I know what this is."

"But you don't. You don't at all," he says, taking the stairs two at a time before coming to stand directly in front of me.

His hands close around my cheeks as he forces my face upwards.

"I'm not good for you, Kimber. You should turn around and walk away from me right now." He sighs. "But for the fucking life of me, I can't let you do it."

"Then I won't." I don't need to consider my response.

I know what I want.

I want him...

"There's no future with me." His words carry a heavy punch yet somehow don't seem to deter me in the least.

"Then I'll take the present." I hold his gaze, the deep gray ocean of his eyes drawing me into their depths until I feel like I can't breathe.

He hits me with an almost pained expression before his mouth closes down on mine, his kiss drowning out everything into the background. It's terrifying how much I want this man. Terrifying, yet something I know I could never fight against.

He may not be able to promise me anything but one fact remains true...

This man *will* change my life.

*This man is already changing my life.*

****

"Do you need anything before I head out, Jane?" I walk behind the bar, sliding my credit cards receipt into my daily folder for management.

"No hon, I think we're good. Has Donna got her station covered?" she asks, sliding a drink across the bar to one of the customers before turning back to me, tucking her highlighted brown bob behind her ears.

"She does," I confirm, grabbing my jacket and bag from under the bar before sliding them on.

"Then I'll see you Thursday." She nods,

giving me a small wave as I step out from behind the bar.

I no more than step outside before my cell phone buzzes to life in my hand, Garrett's name flashing across the screen for the third time today. Letting out a deep exhale, I know I'm going to have to answer it or he will just keep calling.

"What, Garrett?" I snap the moment I press the phone to my ear.

"Everything okay?" His voice bleeds with kindness which is so clearly forced.

"Everything is fine. What do you need?" I sigh, doing very little in the way of hiding my annoyance.

"I miss you. I just wanted to hear your voice."

"Garrett, we've already talked about this. You can't keep calling me. We aren't together anymore."

"That doesn't mean I don't care about you," he interjects.

"No, but it does mean that you don't have any right to continue to harass me." I stop next to a grassy area just a few yards from the restaurant, dropping my book bag onto the ground next to me.

"Is that how you see it?" His tone turns clipped.

"How do you see it? You call me constantly, text me at least once a day, usually multiple times, and for God's sake, Garrett, you flew across the country to see me without so much as a phone call to let me know beforehand."

"We're worried about you." He seethes, his voice going up at least three notches.

"We?" I spit, my frustration mounting.

"As in myself, Dan, and Pat."

"I should have known. Of course, this has to involve my parents'."

"What's that supposed to mean? We all care about you, Kimber."

"Yeah, I can tell. You care about me so much that not one of you can support the decisions I've made or respect what I ask of you. Sounds to me like you care about the fact that I am no longer able to be controlled."

"No one is trying to control you, Kim."

"It's Kimber," I yell, jumping in surprise when I feel the phone pulled out of my hand, turning just in time to see Decklan press it to his ear.

"Stop calling her, asshole, or you're gonna have me to fucking deal with," he threatens, immediately hitting the end button before extending the phone back towards me.

"There. That should get him off your back for a while." He smiles.

"What...what are you doing here?" I gape at him, completely caught off guard by not only his appearance but also by what he just did.

"I was in the area. Thought I'd say hi."
He snakes his arm around my waist and pulls
me into him, dropping a kiss on my lips before
pulling back. "Let me guess, the ex who has no
idea how to pleasure a woman." He hovers
just inches from my face, a slow smirk pulling
up the corner of his mouth.

"Garrett, yes." I sigh, sliding my phone
into the back pocket of my jeans before raising
my hands to rest on his chest. "My parents'
put him up to it, no doubt. They can't stand
the fact that for once in my life I am doing
what I want and not what they expect me to
do."

"Hey." He tips my face upwards,
nudging me under the chin. "Fuck them." I
can't help but smile at his words.

"Just like that huh?" I laugh.

"Just like that."

"Now what are you really doing here? I
know you didn't come all this way just to hang
up on my ex-boyfriend." I take a step back,
retrieving my bag from the ground.

"I came down with Gavin. His mom is
having her monthly Tuesday night spaghetti
dinner. Thought I'd see how you felt about
Italian."

"Are you inviting me to Gavin's parents'
house?" I cock my head to the side.

"I am." His smile deepens. "It's a

tradition at the Porter household, and you'd be doing me a huge favor by saving me from the likes of his cousin Tracy."

"Tracy huh?" I raise my eyebrow, throwing him a curious look.

"She grew up with me and Gavin. I think she's still convinced I am going to marry her one day." He lets out a light laugh.

"Who knows, maybe you will," I tease, nudging him playfully.

"What do say? Save me for an evening?" He hits me with the most pathetic sad face he can muster.

"Now how can I say no to that face?" I laugh. "I have to head back to my room first and change," I say, assuming it's a pretty casual affair considering he's sporting his usual faded jeans, a fitted black t-shirt, and leather jacket.

"Come on, I'll give you a ride." He takes my hand and pulls me in the direction of his bike which I now see is parked directly across the street from the diner.

I must have walked right past him and not even realized it, too busy dealing with Garrett to really pay attention to anything else going on around me.

****

"So this is where you live?" Decklan

follows me inside of my empty dorm room, closing the door behind him.

"It's not much but it's home," I say, looking around the small square space that is packed with two beds, a desk, and more clothes and shoes scattered around the room than two people could ever possibly need.

"Harlee," I explain, pointing to the mess of clothing. "She's in class right now."

"No inspiration?" Decklan doesn't acknowledge my comment, immediately honing in on the easel and blank canvas sitting in the corner of the room.

"It's my final project for the semester. I'm supposed to paint a self-portrait." I shrug, stepping up next to him. "Or rather a portrait of how I view myself. I'm just not quite sure there's anything there to paint." I don't realize the statement until it's already left my mouth.

"What do you mean?" He turns curious eyes on me.

"I don't know." I briefly meet his gaze before turning back to the canvas. "Sometimes I'm just not sure who I am: the girl I want to be or the person my parents' made me."

Grabbing my chin, he turns my face towards him, his gray eyes burning into mine.

"I think you know exactly who you are. You're just afraid to let her out." He pulls my body flush with his, dropping a deep kiss to my mouth.

"Beauty." His lips trail down my jawline, dropping to my neck as he pushes my jacket from my shoulders. "Strength." He tugs the hem of my shirt upward and discards it to the floor before reaching around and unclasping my bra. "Sex." He hisses against my mouth as he pops open the button of my jeans.

"You just have to let yourself see the person I see." He lifts me up, almost immediately depositing me on top of my bed.

I lift up slightly to allow him to peel my jeans and panties away, leaving me completely bare in front of him.

"I'm not sure that person exists."

"Oh, she's in there." He lets out a controlled exhale, dropping his lips to my stomach. "And she's fucking driving me insane." He growls, trailing kisses downward until his face settles between my legs and he nips at my sensitive flesh.

"All I want to do is taste her." He flicks his tongue against my clit causing me to jump slightly. "Feel her quiver beneath me." He flicks again, this time with more force causing a deep moan to escape my throat.

"Fuck, Kimber." His breath is hot on my skin as he continues his slow assault, torturing me with each flicker of his tongue. "That's it, baby." He breathes, applying more pressure as his movements become more purposeful, pulling my body to a height of pleasure it's never before experienced.

I've never done anything like this. While it leaves me so completely exposed and vulnerable, Decklan has a way of making me feel confident and sexy. It allows me to explore the sensation of pleasure coursing through me without judgment.

"Decklan." I arch my back and cry out as an orgasm hits me out of nowhere, building deep within me until I feel like my body is about to split apart beneath his skilled tongue.

He slows his movements, not stopping until he is sure he has pulled every last bit of pleasure from me that he can; my body literally trembling beneath him.

Standing, he grabs my legs and twists, flipping me to my stomach with next to no effort. Securing his hands at the base of my knees he tugs me downward until my feet are on the floor, my backside perched upward.

I hear the rustle of fabric and the rip of the condom wrapper before his massive erection settles against me from behind. Sliding the tip up and down, making sure I'm ready for him. When he finally enters me on a deep thrust, I cry out, my voice muffled against the blanket beneath me.

Gripping it tightly against my face, I let out another deep moan when he rears back and thrusts inside of me again. He goes so deep I swear I can feel him everywhere. His fingers tighten around my hips as he works up a steady rhythm, pumping in and out of me so forcefully that I can feel the mattress sliding against the frame beneath me.

"You better be ready for me, baby." He groans behind me, his movements becoming less controlled with each moment that passes. "Fuck you feel so good."

The slow build that has been working its way back in with each thrust suddenly boils to the surface, the sound of him behind me making it impossible to hold it in any longer. I bunch the blanket tightly in my fingers and scream into the fabric, my entire body going rigid as my second orgasm waves over me with so much intensity I can barely control the quiver running through my body.

"Fuuuuck." I hear Decklan groan behind me as he lets go of his release as well, slamming into me so frantically I know his must be just as intense.

Several long moments pass before he finally slows to a stop and pulls out, pulling me up into his arms. Dropping his face into the crook of my neck, he kisses my flesh, his arms wrapping tightly around my torso.

"What are you doing to me?" He breathes into my hair.

"I could ask you the same question," I get out weakly, turning in his embrace.

"We should go." He lays a gentle kiss to

my lips. "Gavin hates when I leave him alone with his family for too long." He laughs lightly.

"Or we could stay." I take a step backward towards the bed, pulling him along with me.

"You're insatiable." He grins, taking another step with me.

"I mean, we can just leave then." I tease, sliding onto the mattress, putting my entire body on display for him.

"Maybe we have a little more time." He gives me a wicked smile, his eyes holding so much promise. I can already feel my body tightening from the anticipation of what I know is to come.

# Chapter Twelve

## **Decklan**

"You're late." Gavin opens the door and hits me a stern look. A look that completely disappears when he realizes I'm not alone.

"Well hello, Kimber." He gives her a wide smile, opening the door further to allow us both to pass through.

"Is that Decklan?" I hear Rosie, Gavin's mom, before her petite frame pops around the corner, hitting me with a wide smile. "There he is." She crosses the space towards me, wrapping her arms around my waist.

"How's it going, Rosie?" I ask when she finally releases me and steps back to give me the once over.

"Oh you know, trying to keep all these hooligans under control." She sighs, pushing her auburn hair away from her face. "Who's this?" She turns wide eyes on Kimber when she finally registers her semi-hiding behind me.

"Rosie, this is Kimber. Kimber, this is Rosie, Gavin's mom."

"Oh dear, I'm practically mother to all the strays in this neighborhood." She hits me a playful wink before turning her attention back to Kimber.

"It's very nice to meet you, Rosie." Kimber steps forward to take Rosie's extended hand. "I hope I'm not imposing."

"Good heavens, girl, of course not; the more the merrier. That's how we operate around here, isn't that right boys?" She flashes her gaze between me and Gavin. "Besides, it will be nice to have another lady here tonight. Save me from all the testosterone floating around."

Kimber and Rosie laugh in unison, and I can visibly see Kimber relax next to me. She never said it on the way over but I got the impression she was very nervous about coming here tonight. I knew she'd be fine as soon as she met Rosie.

Everyone loves Rosie. She was like a second mother to all of Gavin's friends growing up, including me. Had she not let me stay here my senior year of high school, it's likely I would never have graduated and who knows where I would be now. I am one hundred percent aware that I owe her more than I will ever be able to repay her.

"Well come on you lot, dinner is almost ready," she says before turning her attention to Kimber once more. "You can come with me, let these boys do what boys do." She laughs.

Kimber gives me a small smile and then follows Rosie down the hall towards the kitchen, disappearing from view within seconds.

"What the fuck?" Gavin turns to me the moment we're alone.

"What?"

"You brought her here?" He takes a hard look at my face, clearly trying to place what the hell is going on with me.

"It's just dinner. Besides, I thought it might be nice to have something appealing to look at instead of your ugly ass." I bump my shoulder roughly into his as I head into the living room to my right, tossing my jacket down on the back of the couch.

"Ha. Ha." He crosses his arms in front of his chest, leaning into the wide arc doorway. "You must really like this girl," he observes, his smile spreading.

"Don't do that," I warn.

"Do what?" He fakes innocence.

"Don't make this something it's not. It's not a big deal." I collapse down onto the couch.

"Uh huh." Gavin's smile seems permanently attached to his fucking face, and for some reason, it kind of pisses me off. "I don't know why you're so hell bent on putting on a show, Deck. We may not be blood, but we are brothers. You don't have to front where I'm concerned."

"I'm not." Even as the words come out I know they're bullshit, but I say them anyway.

Truth is, I'm not ready to let this be more than it is. Kimber's a phase. For whatever reason, I need her right now. Right now, not forever. I'll bore of her soon enough and then finally be able to shake the hold she seems to have on me.

"Say whatever makes you sleep better at night, dude, but I fucking know you. Whether you want to admit it or not, that girl is changing you. And for the record—" He cuts me off when I start to interject, "—I think that's a good thing."

I open my mouth to respond but then immediately close it when Rosie's voice filters through the house.

"Dinner's ready." She hollers down the hall before yelling up the stairs as well.

Pushing into a stand, I throw one more warning glare at Gavin, making sure he knows that if he tries any bullshit tonight I won't hesitate to take his ass out, before heading towards the dining room.

****

## <u>Kimber</u>

It's so refreshing to see Decklan like this, relaxed and more at ease than I've seen him before. It's clear by the interactions happening around the Porter dinner table, Decklan is very much a part of this family, and I get the impression that is something that means a great deal to him.

I hide my smile behind my napkin when I look up to see Tracy, Gavin's teenage cousin, sitting across from Decklan, her elbow resting on the table, her cheek propped up on her fist as she gazes dreamily in his direction.

He clearly notices, throwing me a playful side glance when he sees I notice as well. It's innocent, and honestly, I can't say I blame her. I would probably be doing the same thing if I were her. Decklan is beyond gorgeous. Any girl would have to be blind not to be physically drawn to him.

"So, Kimber, what is it that you do, hon?" Rosie cuts into my thoughts, pulling my attention to her.

"I'm actually a freshman at the

University of Oregon." I smile politely, trying not to show just how much I hate being put on the spot.

It's bad enough that Decklan's eyes are on me, but to have Gavin, his mother, two cousins, two uncles, sister and brother-in-law all staring at me makes me feel squeamish. I have to consciously make sure I don't fidget under their gazes.

"My niece Cecelia studies there, something to do with the brain." Rosie laughs when she clearly blanks on what it's called.

"Psychology, Mom." Gavin shakes his head on a laugh.

"That's it, Psychology. What do you study there, dear?"

"Art," I answer, waiting for the familiar looks of disapproval I am used to seeing when I tell someone I am majoring in something so impractical.

To my surprise, not one person looks at me like that.

"That's wonderful. Mr. Porter always loved the Arts. God bless his soul. He took me to this old ratty gallery for our first date. I didn't know anything about art at the time. Listening to him talk about it was like listening to someone speak a foreign language, but oh how I loved to watch the excitement on his face as he tried to explain it to me. I think I fell in love with him that very first night." She smiles fondly at the memory. "Do you know what you want to do after you graduate?"

"I'd actually like to own an Art Gallery," I admit. "As much as I love to paint, I appreciate others work far beyond my own. I can't imagine doing anything more rewarding than helping launch careers of new artists and making sure the world has the opportunity to view their work."

"I think that sounds incredible. Mr. Porter would have really liked you." She turns her attention to Decklan. "She's a special one. Don't you go mucking it up."

I can't help the smile that takes over my face when Decklan laughs and nods at Rosie.

The conversation continues to flow throughout dinner but thankfully stays off of me for the most part; besides the occasional question about West Virginia or my parents', which I manage to brush over seamlessly.

By the time Rosie excuses herself to the kitchen to get dessert, I feel more comfortable than I ever remember feeling at my parents' dinner table. It's clear how loving and supportive this family is, and I can't help but feel envious of Gavin in that regard. He's extremely lucky.

"Thank you for inviting me." I turn my attention to Decklan for the first time in a while.

He gives me a stiff nod but doesn't speak. I can immediately tell something's off. Beads of sweat have formed across his forehead, and his skin is extremely flushed. He takes a deep inhale and lets it out slowly, a small tremor running through him.

"Decklan, are you okay?" I ask, resting my hand on his shoulder which he immediately shakes off.

"I'm fine." He abruptly pushes away from the table, his unexpected action causing me to jump slightly.

Crossing through the dining room, he disappears down the hall before I can really even process what's happening. Just moments later I hear the front door open and close. Not sure if I should follow him or just stay put, I sit conflicted for several long seconds before finally deciding to check on him.

Just as I push my chair back to stand, Gavin halts my movements.

"Don't," he says, pulling my gaze to him. "He'll be fine." His voice is hushed and barely audible over the other various conversations floating around the room. "He just needs a minute."

"What's wrong with him?" I lean forward, trying to keep my voice down.

"It's just a headache, you know from the accident," he says, my stomach twisting slightly at his words.

"What accident?" I ask, obviously having never heard this before.

"Nothing, forget about it." He tries to play if off like it's not a big deal, but I can see right through his failed attempt.

"What accident, Gavin?" I try again but am cut off when Rosie reappears carrying a large glass dish, a perfect looking double layered chocolate cake displayed on top.

"Alright, here it is," she sings, setting it in the center of the table.

As much as I don't want to appear rude, I can't just sit here and eat cake knowing that Decklan is outside in pain. Despite Gavin's advice to leave him be, I politely excuse myself from the table, feeling Gavin's eyes follow me as I cross the room.

I push my way outside moments later, the cool evening air feeling perfect on my heated skin. It takes only seconds to locate Decklan, sitting on the bottom step slumped over, his head dropped to his knees.

"Decklan?" I say his name hesitantly, watching his body go stiff the moment my voice reaches his ears.

"Go back inside, Kimber." His voice is pained.

"Are you okay?" I ask, ignoring his request.

"I said go the fuck back inside, Kimber," he growls, his hands going into his hair as he straightens his posture.

I hesitate for a moment before disregarding his statement.

"No," I insist, my tone absolute.

Climbing to the bottom of the three-step stone staircase, I step directly in front of Decklan and crouch down to his level.

"Not until you tell what I can do to help you," I say, putting my hand under his chin to force his face upwards.

"There's nothing you can fucking do." I suck in a ragged breath when his glossed over gray eyes find mine, the pain behind them so evident. "Fuck." He drops his head slightly, clearly fighting through the pain.

Not sure what else to do, I drop my knees onto the concrete landing and wrap my arms around his neck, securing him against me. I know it does nothing for the pain he's clearly feeling, but I'm just trying to bring him even the smallest bit of comfort. He doesn't return my embrace, but he doesn't reject it either. Instead, he simply rocks in my arms as I gently trail my fingertips across the back of his neck and across his shoulders.

When his body relaxes slightly and his arms close around me, pulling me into his chest, I know that the pain has finally passed. Though by the tremble in his hands, I can tell the effects of that pain are still very much present.

"I'm sorry." He breathes, burying his face in the crook of my neck as he holds me tightly.

"Don't be," I say, my fingers continuing to gently move across back.

"I shouldn't have yelled at you like that."

"What happened?" I pull back slightly to meet his gaze.

"Just a headache, it's nothing." He tucks my hair behind my ear, trailing the back of his hand gently down my cheek.

"From the accident?" I ask, seeing him visibly stiffen at my words. "Why didn't you tell me you were in some kind of accident? Was it bad?" I ask, just trying to understand what would bring on such intense pain when minutes earlier he was fine.

"It's nothing. It was a long time ago." He gives me a vague reply, clearly not wanting to talk about it.

"Is that how you got this?" I ask, trailing my fingers gently across the scar that runs across his left temple.

He reaches up and immediately halts my movements, wrapping his hand around mine.

"I should probably get you home." The abruptness of his statement catches me off guard.

"Oh, okay," I say, letting my hand drop away. "I'm sorry if I pushed too hard. I just want to understand," I try to explain.

"It's fine, really." He pushes into a stand, lifting me to my feet as he does. "I'm going to tell Rosie goodbye and then we'll go," he says, turning and walking back inside the house without another word.

****

"What are you doing Friday?" Decklan asks, pulling the helmet from my head to rest it on the seat of the motorcycle just moments after arriving at my dorm.

"I don't have anything planned," I answer hesitantly, still not sure what the hell happened at the Porter's house or how he can filter between hot and cold so rapidly.

One minute he's all about me: touching me, throwing heated glances in my direction. The next he's treating me like a nuisance; someone not worthy of sharing his pain, and I don't just mean physical. He tries to hide it, but I can still see it. He's buried, it but that doesn't mean it doesn't show through.

"We're throwing our annual Halloween party at *Deviants*." He cuts into my thoughts, taking my hand as he walks me towards my building. "You and your friends should come. Everyone dresses up, well besides me." He laughs lightly. "It's a pretty good time."

We get to the front steps of my dorm building before I finally respond.

"Sounds fun." I turn to face him, not as excited as I normally would be given that things still feel off between us.

"So I'll see you then?" he asks, trailing the pad of his thumb across my chin.

"Yeah. I'll see you then," I say, pushing up onto my tiptoes to lay a brief kiss to his lips before turning and disappearing inside.

As much as I want to see him again, I just don't know how good of an idea it is to keep this going. I thought I knew what I signed up for with Decklan, and he's been perfectly clear on what this is for him. But even still, deep down I really just thought it would be different. Realizing that it won't be might prove to be more than I am capable of handling.

# Chapter Thirteen

## <u>Kimber</u>

"That's what you're wearing?" I gawk at Angel who emerges from the bathroom dressed in nothing more than a white corset and a white skirt so short if she bends over her entire backside will be on full display.

"Don't worry, I'm gonna wear a halo and wings, too." She gives me a mischievous smile.

"And that's gonna somehow make the fact that you're practically naked okay?" I laugh, shaking my head at her.

"I hate to tell you, but you don't have much room to talk." She gestures to my police costume.

The skimpy number consists only of a

skin tight navy blue dress that stops several inches above my knee, a thick black belt with handcuffs, and a matching hat that sits on top of my straight sexy hair that Harlee spent an hour perfecting. Add on the black heels I borrowed from Angel and I hate to admit she might be right.

In my defense, I borrowed this from Harlee and it's by far the least slutty one she had to offer. I don't have a ton of money to sink into something like a Halloween costume. Not when I have to worry about things like being able to eat and afford my supplies for school.

"Does it look okay?" I crunch my forehead, suddenly very concerned that maybe I can't pull this look off.

"Um incredible," Harlee chimes in from the vanity as she places the final piece of her costume on her head: a feather headband to complete her flapper girl costume. "Trust me, girl, no way that hunk of yours is going to be able to take his eyes off you tonight." She raises her eyebrows up and down suggestively.

"I call dibs on his hot bartender friend." Angel pulls my attention back to her. "I mean, yummy."

"You can't call dibs over my dibs," Harlee interjects. "Mine." She pins her eyes directly on Angel.

"If I had to guess, I think he'd be okay

with you two sharing." I laugh when both girls turn wide eyes on me.

"Who are you and what did you do with my sweet little Kimber?" Harlee laughs, crossing her arms in front of herself.

"I buried her out back. I like this version so much better." I laugh, snagging my cell phone from the bed.

"Me, too." Angel drops an arm over my shoulder. "Well, ladies, you ready," she asks, the last part coming out as an excited squeal.

"Ready." I smile, letting out a nervous exhale.

****

*Deviants* is busier than I have ever seen it. There is a line of elaborately dressed individuals almost wrapping the building. Angel has to park two blocks away because there is not one parking spot anywhere remotely close.

I'm almost worried we won't be able to get in until I see Gavin step outside just as we approach the front entrance. His timing couldn't be better.

It isn't until we get within a couple of feet that I see his attire. He's dressed in a ripped white t-shirt, fake blood-soaked down the front, his face painted to look like he is no longer among the living.

"Don't arrest me, officer, I swear I'm innocent." He holds his hands up on a laugh the moment his eyes land on me.

"Somehow I doubt that." I return his laugh, stopping directly in front of him.

Holding a cigarette loosely between his lips, his eyes trail down the two women who stop next to me. "Ladies, nice to see you again." He gives Harlee a brilliant smile, and I hear her soft exhale of excitement next to me.

"Zombie." I point to his outfit.

"Easiest costume there is." He tilts his head back on a laugh when I crinkle my nose. "I take it you're not a fan?"

"Of dead people walking around trying to eat me, not so much." I shake my head on a laugh. "This is crazy," I observe, gesturing to the amount of people waiting to get in.

"Oh just wait." He laughs. "Best night of the year."

"Is Decklan inside?" I ask as he pulls a lighter from his pocket and lights the tip of his cigarette, taking a long drag and exhaling before answering.

"I think he's upstairs." He takes another drag. "You're welcome to head on in," he says, holding up his index finger as he digs into his back pocket with the opposite hand, pulling out yellow wristbands just moments later.

"I'm good, I'm not drinking," I say, shaking my head.

"Ladies?" He offers Harlee and Angel each one which they happily accept.

Turning towards the bulky guy sitting at the door, he gestures to the three of us and nods, the bouncer nodding back.

"You're good to head on in."

"Thanks, Gavin." I smile, nodding as I head towards the front door.

"I think I'm gonna hang out here for a minute," Harlee calls behind me, halting both mine and Angel's steps. I turn my head to see a wide smile on her face. "I won't be long," she reassures me, winking.

Shaking my head, I grab Angel's forearm as she starts to object and drag her inside behind me, my steps faltering the moment the door closes behind us. It takes me a moment to take it all in.

The entire room is done up like some freak show haunted fun house. Black lights and strobe lights have taken the place of the normal dim bar lighting. Crazy mirrors line the exterior walls, and there are at least three, that I can see, life-size clowns that remind me of Pennywise from the movie 'It'.

"Shit, they really get into this." Angel steps up next to me, looking around the room.

"That they do," I agree. "I'm gonna go try to find Decklan, are you okay for a minute?" I ask, not really wanting to leave her alone but also not able to fight how badly I am dying to see him right now.

We haven't spoken since Tuesday when he dropped me off after dinner at the Porters house, and I haven't felt right about anything since then. I tried texting him a couple of times but have gotten no response. A part of me even considered not coming tonight fearing maybe he doesn't want to see me.

"Yeah, yeah, go." Angel shoos me with her hands. "I'm gonna grab a drink and scour the room for some hotties." She winks.

"I'll be back," I say, turning as I push my way through the thick crowd of witches, vampires, devils, and other various disguises.

Not sure if I can just go up, I hesitate at the edge of the bar, catching the attention of a short dark haired girl who crosses towards me the moment she sees me.

"Can I get ya something hon?" she asks, reaching into the cooler not feet from me to grab a beer, immediately sliding it across the bar to a man on the other side before turning back to me.

"Is Decklan upstairs?" I ask, not missing the recognition that crosses her face the moment the question leaves my mouth.

"Kimber?" Her lips turn up in a wide smile when I nod. "You can go on up." She pulls the door open and gestures up the stairs without a moment's hesitation. Her action leads me to believe that maybe he informed her to send me up when I arrived.

The thought makes me feel just a tiny bit better but doesn't fully calm the butterflies in my stomach still flapping around nervously.

"Tell him to get his ass down here if you don't mind." She nods before letting the door close behind me.

It takes only seconds for me to climb the narrow staircase, the dark wood of Decklan's door directly in front of me before I even have a moment to figure out what I'm going to say or how I'm going to act.

This whole thing is so new to me. I really have no idea how to conduct myself. Do I act entitled like a girlfriend? Should I go back downstairs and wait for him to find me?

Before I can overthink it too much, I reach my hand up and knock lightly on the door, Decklan's voice sounding just moments later.

"What?" he yells from inside, aggravation evident in his tone.

"It's Kimber," I get out weakly.

I stand in complete silence for what feels like several long moments but is likely just a few short seconds, wondering if he even heard me before I finally hear him again.

"Come in."

Pushing my way inside, it takes my eyes a moment to adjust to the dark room, the only light provided by the street lamp outside. I close the door softly behind me before spotting Decklan sitting on the couch, a glass in his hand, a near empty bottle of whiskey on the coffee table in front of him.

"Hey," I say softly, not sure exactly what I'm walking into.

"Hey." His response is casual as he leans forward and refills the glass in his hand, slugging back the contents seconds later.

"What are you doing up here?" I ask, slowly crossing the space towards him.

"I just needed a few." He lets out a deep exhale.

"Do you want me to go?" I ask, stopping just feet from where he's sitting.

"No." His answer is instant. "That's the last thing I want," he says, for the first time taking in my attire as I step directly into the light filtering in through the window.

He takes a ragged inhale, and even in the darkness I can see the desire form behind his incredible eyes.

"You like?" I ask, holding my arms out to the side so he can get the full view.

"What do you think?" He grabs my hand and pulls me into his lap.

"I'm guessing yes?" I laugh, feeling him grow hard beneath me.

"You guessed fucking right." He growls, pulling my face down to his.

The moment our lips meet, he pulls me

in deeper, the taste and smell of whiskey invading my senses in an instant. As much as I hate whiskey, I have to admit I love the way it tastes on him.

"You're killing me, Kimber." He groans, pulling my bottom lip into his mouth.

"You say that like it's a bad thing," I get out on a pant when his lips find my neck and he nibbles at my flesh.

"It is a bad thing. A very bad thing." He nips roughly at the base of my neck before tossing me backward onto the couch.

I don't have time to react before he's hovering over me, popping the buttons of my costume open one at a time, his eyes remaining focused on each inch of flesh as it's exposed. Within seconds, the dress is laying open and his hands are trailing across the bare flesh of my abdomen.

"You're all I can think about." He groans, dipping his fingers inside my panties to find me already ready for him. "Fuck." He shoves two fingers roughly inside causing a cry of pleasure to rip from my throat.

"I don't want to think about you. I don't want to want you, Kimber." His breathing becomes more rapid as he begins pumping his fingers inside of me. "But fuck me, I can't shake you."

"Then maybe you should stop trying." My words come out shaky and barely break the surface.

"Maybe you're right." He abruptly pulls his hand away, his fingers tangling in the thin material of my panties, and in one hard tug, the fabric tears away.

I want to object, curse at him for ruining the only pair of underwear I have here, but I am too turned on by the action to follow through.

"I want you like this all night, Kimber." He tosses the thin ripped material to the side. "Bare and ready for me." He slides his index finger back inside of me before pulling it out and raising it to his lips.

He sucks it into his mouth, moaning as my flavor hits his tongue. The action is so erotic that the self-consciousness I may normally feel doesn't even attempt to make an appearance.

Slowly he begins buttoning my costume back up, sliding it down over my bare ass as he pulls me up from the couch.

"Decklan," I object, feeling the familiar ache in my belly any time he's near. An ache I need him to satisfy.

"Patience." He gives me a wicked grin. "I want you to get a small taste of how I feel every single time I'm around you. I want you to feel exposed, vulnerable, and so completely fucking aroused you can barely think straight. " He breathes against my mouth, dropping a brief kiss to my jaw as he pushes off of the couch, adjusting his erection before taking my hand and pulling me to my feet.

"But," I object, knowing there is no way I can go down there with no panties on.

"When I decide I can no longer take the thought of you just feet from me, bare and wet waiting for me to fuck you." He pauses just next to the door. "Then I'll have my way with you. Not a moment sooner." He kisses me deeply, silencing my lingering objections.

I have no choice but to comply.

How could I ever deny him a request that sends my blood boiling with the heat of his statement?

This man owns me...

There is not one thing I wouldn't do for him right here and now.

# Chapter Fourteen

**<u>Decklan</u>**

What the fuck was I thinking? I wasn't, truth be told. I didn't realize how fucking crazy it would make me knowing Kimber is prancing around in that tight little costume with not a god damn thing underneath.

I think a part of me doubted she would go through with it. Not only did she, but she's owning it, teasing me, using it against me at every turn. I both love it and fucking hate it at the same time.

I haven't been able to take my eyes off of her all night. Not when I'm so aware of how exposed she is right now and that one little bend or lift of her dress and the whole bar would get a peek of what is mine.

Mine?

Even as foreign as that sounds to me, I know there's no denying the possessiveness I feel towards this girl. She fucking is mine whether she knows it or not.

So instead of working or doing anything for that matter, I have found myself for most of the night lounging at the bar watching her and her two friends, one of which Gavin seems to have taken a particular interest in.

I guess it shouldn't surprise me. Gavin is a sucker for tall thin blondes and Harlee, Kimber's roommate is definitely that.

I can't help but smile when I see Kimber crossing the space towards me, purposely avoiding meeting my gaze as she passes by. Reaching out I snake my arm around her waist and pull her towards me, laughing when she lets out a playful squeal.

"And just where do you think you're going?" I shift in the barstool, pulling her small body between my legs.

"Well, there's this really hot guy over there. I thought maybe I'd check it out." She crinkles her nose playfully.

"Careful," I warn, leaning down to suck her bottom lip into my mouth.

She lets out a soft moan, her nails digging into the fabric of my jeans as she squeezes just above my knees, sinking deeper against me.

"Can we go yet?" She whines, pulling back to puff out her bottom lip at me.

"I don't know. I'm rather enjoying myself," I lie, knowing full well the only thing I want to do right now is bury myself between her legs.

"Well, you remember that when I have to leave to take Angel and Harlee home." She crosses her arms in front of her chest.

"You're not staying?" I can't contain the disappointment in my voice no matter how hard I try to mask it.

"I didn't think you'd want me to." She seems surprised by my reaction.

"Come on." I avoid her statement as I push out of the stool, grabbing her hand to pull her behind me.

"Wait, where are we going? I didn't get to go talk to that guy," she objects as I pull her inside the stairwell, slamming the door shut the moment she's inside.

"Fuck that guy. You're fucking mine," I growl, my mouth crashing down on hers as I pull her into me.

She gasps lightly when I lift her, quickly securing her legs around my waist as I begin to climb the stairs, pushing my way inside my apartment within a matter of seconds. Swinging the door closed behind us, I immediately cross the room, depositing her on top of the bed the moment I reach it.

Reaching down, I spread her legs open, taking in a sharp inhale when my eyes meet her bare flesh. It's all I have thought about all night: seeing her, feeling her. This girl has me by the fucking balls, and there's not a fucking thing I can do about it.

Trailing my hand lightly between her legs, I can't fight my smile when she arches her back, pushing into my touch.

"Now, Decklan. Do it now," she whimpers when I press the pad of my thumb against her clit and slowly rotate it.

"Do what now?" I increase the speed of my finger but still keep my pace slow enough that her frustration lingers, wanting her to beg for it.

"Fuck me, Decklan." I can't deny how fucking incredible those words sound coming out of her pretty little mouth.

"You want me to what?" I increase the speed of my hand more, my erection pressing so tightly against my jeans it's past the point of uncomfortable.

I know I'm teasing her, but in the process, I'm fucking torturing myself. Just watching her writhe beneath my touch is enough to drive me beyond the point where I can hold out any longer.

"Fuck," I grind out, dropping my hand away as I tear open my jeans.

I don't bother undressing her further. I love seeing her like this. Her tight little dress squeezing her body just right, her wet pussy exposed and on full display for me. I bite down on my bottom lip, trying to steady my hand as I quickly slide a condom on.

Pulling her ass to the edge of the mattress, I spread her legs wider, taking one last long look before I bury myself deep inside of her.

The initial impact nearly brings me to the brink, and I have to still myself inside of her for a brief moment. Taking a deep breath, I try to reel myself in and get my shit together. I can't let myself lose control that quickly. I need her there with me first.

Crawling up her body, I drag her further up the mattress with me as I go, and settle down on top of her as I drop my lips back down to hers. She feels so fucking incredible around me, I'm afraid any movement will send me over the edge.

Sliding her arms around me, Kimber deepens the kiss as she urges me forward, raising her hips slightly to meet my slow thrust. I pull out and slide slowly back in, trying to keep my movements controlled as I quicken my pace.

It's not long before I feel Kimber's grip start to tighten and her perfect façade falling away. It's in these moments, in the rawness of pleasure, that I see her for who she really is. Wild, untamed, not afraid to take what she wants, and fuck me the most beautiful fucking creature to ever lie beneath me.

My release hits me with so much force that I barely register Kimber's cries as she succumbs to her own pleasure. My stomach cramps tightly, the intensity of my orgasm almost painful as it spills out of me.

****

"Tell me how you got this?" Kimber trails her finger lightly down the scar that lines the side of my skull, the contact causing me to tense slightly. She props herself up on her elbow, her body still tucked into my side as she meets my gaze.

"Hit my head." My answer is generic and void of any emotion. I've perfected that much.

"What happened?" She pushes for more, her eyes full of curiosity.

"It was nothing." I shrug it off, closing my hand around hers to pull her fingers away from the jagged flesh. "Nothing to worry yourself with." I kiss her knuckles before laying her palm flat against my chest.

I can see the hesitation in her eyes, and I know instantly that she wants to ask for more. She studies me for a long moment before finally deciding to let it be. Relaxing back down into my arms, she lays her face against my chest and lets out a slow exhale.

"What's wrong?" I ask, trailing my fingers lightly through her hair.

"I'm not ready to leave," she admits, working slow circles across my stomach with her fingertips.

"Then don't."

"You know I have to." She lets out another sigh.

"You don't have to do anything," I challenge, gently rolling her onto her back as I pin her body beneath mine. "I mean, I could just make you stay," I threaten, dropping my mouth to hers.

"I know you're in there, bitch." A woman's voice I don't instantly recognize suddenly rings through the otherwise empty space followed by a loud series of thumping.

"What the fuck?" I mutter, looking down at Kimber, whose eyes are wide as she stares back at me.

Before I have a chance to react, let alone respond, Kimber yells back, the level of her voice enough to vibrate her chest against mine.

"Twenty more minutes." She laughs at the curious look I give her. "Angel," she whispers.

"Stop it. They're in there getting nasty." I hear another voice I can only assume belongs to Harlee, followed by giggling.

"You know we can hear you." Kimber tries to keep the humor from her voice as the laughter on the other side of the door continues.

Throwing me a sweet smile, I know instantly the moment is over. Silently cursing her friends for their less than stellar timing, I roll to the side, pushing myself out of the bed. Kimber joins me within seconds, frantically searching the floor for her dress which takes her a moment to find given the darkness of the room.

"I'll get it." I shake my head when another round of pounding sounds against the door.

Sliding on my jeans, I don't bother locating my shirt as I cross the space of the room, ripping open the door just as Angel has her hand lifted to knock again.

"Well fuck me." She lets out a loud sigh, her eyes traveling down my bare torso. "Please tell me you have a brother." She squeals when Harlee smacks the back of her arm.

"Trust me, he's not anything like Decklan." Kimber appears suddenly at my side, her comment catching me off guard for a brief moment until I remember the day I had lunch with Mom and Trey. I had completely forgotten she was even there.

Giving me the type of smile that makes

my stomach twist slightly, she pushes up on her tiptoes to lay a brief kiss to my cheek. "I'll call you later." She winks, shoving Harlee and Angel away from the doorframe as she steps into the hall.

"Goodnight, Decklan," Angel sings up the stairs just moments before I hear the noise of the bar filter through the open doorway.

Glancing at the clock, I see it's just after midnight. Knowing we are going to have a hell of a lot to clean up, I decide to get dressed and head back down. If I'm lucky, the place won't be too trashed.

"He's alive." Gavin smiles at me from his stool at the edge of the bar the moment I step through the door.

"What happened to keeping her friends busy?" I grunt, sliding down into the stool next to him before signaling to Val.

She nods, appearing in front of me within seconds with a rocks glass in one hand, a bottle of whiskey in the other. "Where have you been all night?" she asks before Gavin can respond, a teasing undertone apparent in her voice.

"Where do you think he was?" Gavin laughs beside me, draining his glass before taking the bottle from Val and refilling it, then depositing the half empty bottle onto the bar in front of us.

"He's in love." His voice goes up an

octave as he sways next to me.

"I'm not in love," I grunt, draining the contents of my glass in one drink.

"I don't know, boss, even I have to admit I've never seen you act this way before," Val agrees, taking the bottle from my hand after I refill the empty glass in front of me.

"It's called mixing it up. You two should try it sometime." I try to let their comments roll off my back, but even I can't deny the shred of truth they may hold.

Is Kimber really changing me that much?

I know the answer to that question without giving it a second thought.

"Is that what people are calling it these days?" he smarts off.

"You really want to go there?" I throw him a warning glare.

"So defensive." Gavin clicks his tongue off the roof of his mouth.

"And how about you?" I turn towards him. "Since when have you not been able to land a woman you've locked in on?" I give him a knowing smile. "Not going soft are we?"

"Fuck you, Deck. I'm not soft. I'm just sure as hell not going to throw myself at someone who wants to play hard to get, especially when I have so many others begging. That may be a fun game for you, but I don't do games; I fuck." He shoots Val a vicious look when she lets out a loud snort.

"Sorry." She laughs. "But you two kill me." She turns, shaking her head as she walks away.

"What the fuck?" Gavin growls, his eyes still fixed on Val as she leans across the counter to take a customer's order.

"What?" I throw him a curious glance.

"Why'd she laugh like that?" He seems genuinely bothered by Val's reaction.

"Probably because she knows you." I grin, emptying the rest of my drink in one swig.

"What the fuck's that supposed to mean?"

"Nothing." I shake my head, not feeling up to spending the next hour reassuring him that he's not completely losing his touch.

Gavin has always had a way with women, and I'm sure it's grating on him that Harlee hasn't dropped to her knees and begged him to take her. I find the whole situation quite humorous really. It also gives me a welcome distraction from my own current situation.

It's easier to focus on other people's lives than to deal with the fact that mine looks completely foreign to me. For the longest time I have operated the exact same way, and to have someone show up and completely unhinge all of that is fucking unsettling as hell.

I try to convince myself it's nothing, that I will bore of Kimber eventually. But deep down I think I know that's not true.

I think I know she means a hell of a lot more to me than I am willing to admit. Because admitting that gives up the control that I am so desperately clinging to. I can't let myself go down this road. I can't risk hurting her the way I eventually hurt everyone who gets too close to me.

I don't think I could bear to have her look at me with the same disappointment I have seen so many times before. To see pain in her eyes and know I put it there. I think ultimately, that's what scares me the most.

# Chapter Fifteen

## Kimber

"Yes, I know it's been a while." I try my best to muffle my frustration about having the same conversation with my mom yet again.

"Is it so much to ask that you call your parents' from time to time? Honestly, Kimber, did we not raise you better than this?" Her judgmental tone is no less effective thousands of miles away, and I still find myself shrinking slightly.

"Your father is convinced the only way to reason with you is to come to Oregon and put you on a plane himself," she continues.

"I'm not a child. He can't just force me to come home," I object, knowing the last thing I want is for Dan James to show up here.

"You are *our* child, or have you forgotten that?"

"Of course, I haven't. Just because I'm following my own path doesn't mean I love you any less. But this is my life, Mom. You're just going to have to find a way to live with my choices."

"One day, Kimber, you'll have children of your own..."

"And I will love them and teach them. And when they're old enough, I will trust them to choose for themselves and know they will do the right thing because I raised them right," I cut her off.

"It's not always so black and white," she snips, sighing loudly into the phone.

"No, it's not," I agree. "But you know me; have you no faith that I can do this on my own?"

"It's not that," she objects.

"Then what is it? Because from where I'm standing that's exactly what it boils down to, you don't trust me. But here's the good news, you don't have too. I am an adult, and I will make my choices whether you support them or not."

"Kimber."

"I'm not doing this." I look up from my place on the bed, throwing a frustrated glance to Harlee who quietly closes the door behind her as she steps inside the room.

"You're leaving us with very little choice," my mom warns.

"And you're leaving me with very little," I promise, feeling the emotion clog my throat.

I've tried telling my parents' how much their support would mean to me, but it still seems to make no difference. I just don't understand how parents can treat their own child this way. I'd be lying if I said this whole situation doesn't break my heart a little. I want nothing more than to live my life my way and know I have my parents' there to back me every step of the way. No child should ever have to choose between their family and their freedom.

"I have to go, I have class," I lie, not waiting for her response before ending the call, dropping the phone on the mattress in front of me.

"Again?" Harlee drops her bag onto the floor before taking a seat on the edge of my bed.

"It's never ending." I sigh, meeting her sympathetic gaze.

If anyone understands bad parenting it's Harlee, though her situation is so much worse than mine. Her mom died of a drug overdose when she was only ten years old which left her with her drunk of a father until he was sentenced to ten years in prison when she was fifteen. She got taken in by a wealthy aunt after that, but that's all I really know.

"You can't force them to come around. All you can do is live your life for you. Either they'll decide it's better to let you be yourself rather than lose you all together or they won't. Either way, I think you'll be just fine." She gives me a reassuring smile.

"I know. It's just hard." I let out a deep sigh.

"I get it." She pats my leg before pushing up off the bed. "So how are things with lover boy?" I don't object to her abrupt subject change, having no desire to beat the dead horse that is my relationship with my parents'.

"Good." I smile at the thought of Decklan. "Really good actually."

"So things are getting more serious?" I watch her grab her book bag from the floor and cross the space to her own bed before she finally turns her gaze back to me.

"I don't know that I would say that. I mean, it's intense," I admit. "He's intense." I sigh. "And very hard to read."

"How so?" she asks, flopping down onto her mattress as she pulls her bag into her lap.

"I mean, it's amazing when we're together, but I can't seem to get past how closed off he is. Every time I ask him anything personal, he shuts down. Kind of makes me feel unimportant, like I'm not worth sharing things with."

"Give it time," Harlee reassures me. "Some guys just have a really hard time opening up. He'll get there."

"How can you be so sure?"

"Because I've seen the way that man looks at you." Her answer is immediate.

"What do you mean?" Her response makes me curious.

"I can't explain it. It's just something about the way he watches you like you belong to him."

"Is that a good thing?" I laugh, still not sure how I feel about this whole situation.

I'm terrified by how strongly I feel for him over such a short period of time. It seems unnatural to me that after just a few short weeks he has such a hold on me. He's all I can think about; all I dream about. When I'm with him I never want to leave. When I'm not with him, all I want to do is be with him again.

Despite how quickly my feelings for Decklan have formed, I think I'm more worried that I'm just being caught up by a smooth talking playboy that will discard me the moment he's finished with me. The thought leaves me with a sick feeling in the pit of my stomach, and I have to shake off the direction my mind is going.

"I think so," Harlee cuts into my thoughts, pulling my attention back to her.

"Have you heard from him today?" she asks.

"Not today. He's covering the bar this afternoon I think. Why?" I get the feeling there is more to her question than just wanting to know if I have spoken to him.

"Just wondering." She shrugs,

"You sure?" I cock my head to the side, waiting for her to finish pulling out her books and depositing them across the top of the bed before continuing. "Your question wouldn't have anything to do with Gavin would it?" I give her a knowing smile when she meets my gaze.

"He's got me so mixed up," she blurts, blood rushing to her cheeks.

"What's going on?" I ask, having not really spoken to Harlee about Gavin in any real length.

It's been a week and a half since the Halloween party at *Deviants,* and she's only mentioned him a couple of times in front of me. I know she finds him very attractive, but I'm a little confused as to where this reaction is coming from. Clearly something has happened that I have not been made aware of.

"It's nothing." She shakes her head.

"Bull." I hit her with a mischievous smile. "Something happened. Spill." I adjust my position on the bed slightly so that I am facing directly towards her.

"It's really not a big deal." She shrugs.

"We kissed the night of the Halloween party." I can't help but laugh at how she says it. Harlee is usually balls to the wall, says what she thinks, and makes no apology. I've never seen her like this before.

"But then I saw him again after that and well, we may have slept together." She drops her face into her hands.

"What? When?" I ask in shock over her confession. I had no idea any of this was going on.

"Five days ago." She hits me with an apologetic look.

"And you're just now telling me?" I blurt.

"I thought you'd be upset. You know because this thing with Decklan is so new, and I was afraid maybe you thought I'd screw it up by getting mixed up with his friend."

"Are you kidding?" I crinkle my forehead in confusion. "Gavin is not Decklan. Whatever happens between the two of you is solely between you and him. Besides, I think it's awesome," I tack on.

"Well considering I haven't heard from him since then, I'm not so sure."

"Is that why you were asking if I had heard from Decklan?" I ask, finally piecing together the dots.

"I called the bar earlier and Gavin answered." She shakes her head like she's ashamed of her actions. "I don't have his cell number but I gave him mine." She tries to explain. "Anyways, I asked him if he wanted to hang out, maybe grab a bite to eat, and he told me he had to cover the bar tonight. When I suggested maybe coming up to keep him company he completely shot down the idea which obviously made me question if he was really telling me the truth."

"Only one way to find out." I grab my cell, scrolling through my contacts until I find the number to *Deviants*.

Pressing send, it rings three times before Decklan answers.

"Hey." I blush slightly in spite of myself.

Just hearing him over the phone sends my heart galloping inside of my chest.

"Hey." I can hear the smile in his voice as he responds.

"I just wanted to call and make sure you weren't going stir crazy." I laugh, picking at the blanket on my bed.

Considering it's a Wednesday night and from what I have gathered they are pretty slow through the week, I figured this was a justifiable excuse for calling.

"Well, I probably would be if I didn't have Matt here talking my fucking ear off." I can tell by how he says this that I'm not the only person he's saying it to.

I laugh when I hear Matt, one of

*Deviants* part-time bartenders, yell something in the background.

"Shut the fuck up," Decklan responds, though I have no idea what he's responding to.

"Just tell Gavin to entertain him." I laugh, getting the information I need without actually having to ask for it.

"I would if his ass was here." I hear Matt again in the background. "Dude shut up or I'm going to cut your ass off and send you home," Decklan warns.

"That's surprising." I ignore the side conversation going on with Matt and focus on the purpose of my call. "I thought he never left." I laugh, throwing Harlee a quick glance who is clearly listening to every word and is not very pleased to hear Gavin isn't there.

"He rarely does, unless there's a woman involved." His response causes my stomach to twist slightly, being the last thing I want to tell Harlee.

"Good to know." I laugh it off. "Well, I'm gonna let you get back to it. I just wanted to say hi."

"Okay." I can once again hear the smile in his voice. "I'll call you later."

"You better," I playfully warn.

He waits for my response, laughing lightly on the other end before finally ending the call.

Dropping my cell down onto the

mattress in front of me, I don't have a chance to say even a word before Harlee pushes off her bed.

"I fucking knew it. That fucking liar." She paces the room, clearly trying to reign in her emotions.

"Maybe it's not what you think" I interject.

"Bullshit." She spins towards me. "What did Decklan say? Where is he?" she asks, seeming to already know.

"He didn't say specifically," I answer truthfully.

"But he's not there right?"

"No," I confirm.

"See, I just don't get it. If he doesn't want to hang out with me why not just say that? Why lie to me about having to cover the bar?"

"I don't know." I hate that I can't find something else to say.

"Fuck it." She throws her hands up. "He wants to play that way, fine. Two can play that game." She crosses towards the closet, ripping the door open the moment she reaches it.

"What are you doing?" I watch as she shuffles through her clothes, finally pulling out a pair of jeans and a skimpy black top, throwing them across her bed.

"I'm going out," she answers like it should be obvious. "His actions have made it very clear what he wanted from me. I'm not about to sit around and mope over a man who clearly just used me for a piece of ass." She slides off her long sleeve t-shirt and tosses it onto the floor.

"Where are you going?"

"Angel and Jess are hitting up *Metros* tonight. I think I'll join them." She slides off her jeans, having absolutely no shame about stripping in front of me. "You should come with us," she tacks on.

"No thanks. I've got to work on my project tonight. At this rate I'm never going to complete it on time," I say, referring to the self-portrait that I've been working on for nearly a week and have started from scratch on three times now.

"Suit yourself." She flips her long blonde hair over her shoulder as she turns, disappearing into the bathroom.

Shaking my head, I push off of the bed and slide on my shoes before crossing the short distance of the room. Slipping on my jacket, I grab my bag from the floor before pushing open the door and stepping into the hallway, closing it quietly behind me.

There are so many things I would rather be doing tonight, but time is not on my side right now. With my school and work schedule, I'll be lucky if I can manage to turn in something even remotely acceptable.

At least, the labs are open twenty-four hours a day, and I can spend as much time as I need trying to finish it. I have flown through all my other assignments with next to no issue, creating some of my best work in the three short months I've been here, but for whatever reason I can't seem to pound this one out. Every time I try I just end creating some generic piece that looks like I just slapped a sloppy picture of my face on the canvas, and that's not the point.

It's not about painting my face or my physical appearance at all for that matter. It's about painting myself as I see me, from the inside out. Problem is, I'm not sure that I know what that me looks like anymore.

# Chapter Sixteen

## **<u>Kimber</u>**

"What are you doing here?" The surprise in my voice is clear.

I can't help the wide smile that stretches across my face at the sight of Decklan. His incredible body dressed in his usual fitted t-shirt, dark jeans and black leather jacket, his messy hair falling haphazardly in front of his impossibly handsome face.

Oh dear Lord, please help me. I swear he gets better looking each time I see him as if that were even possible. Just the sight of him makes my legs tremble slightly beneath my weight.

I had no idea he was coming out this

way today, let alone that I would find him standing outside waiting for me to get off work.

"I missed you." His statement causes my chest to constrict tightly as I cross the sidewalk to where he's leaning casually against his bike just outside of *Lovett's*.

"Well, here I am," I tease.

Grabbing the front of his shirt, I pull his face down to mine. The moment our lips meet the same familiar tingle surges through my body. It starts at the point of contact and slowly spreads until I can feel the effects of him everywhere.

He slows my advances, smiling against my mouth just seconds before he pulls back and stares down at me with those incredible gray eyes of his.

"Do you have a couple hours free? I want to show you something." He runs the pad of his thumb along my chin causing me to take a sharp inhale.

"Of course," I agree instantly. "But should I change?" I gesture to my long black top and skinny jeans, partnered with a pair of black flats.

"You're perfect." He drops another brief kiss to my lips. "Besides, it's only going to be us." His eyes twinkle mischievously.

"What are you up to?" I hit him with a curious look, not able to contain my smile.

"You'll see," he promises, turning to retrieve his motorcycle helmet before depositing it onto my head.

****

"Where are we?" I look up at Decklan who only gives me a wide smile and winks before tangling his fingers with mine and pulling me towards the back of the old brick building in front of us.

"Just come on." He laughs lightly, quickening his pace.

I have no idea where exactly we are, but considering we drove for only a few short minutes to get here I'd say we aren't that far from campus. We are surrounded by at least a handful of other buildings that seem to be set up similarly; all the same, dingy two story brick. There are intersecting sidewalks that connect to form almost a circle around the buildings.

If I had to guess, I would say they are all part of the same thing; similar to a college that is made up of several different buildings only much smaller than that. Despite the fact that it's mid-afternoon, the entire area seems to be completely vacant. Then again it is Sunday, perhaps it's just closed today, whatever this is.

Decklan drops my hand just as we reach the back entrance, pulling a set of keys from his pocket and inserting them into the lock without once looking in my direction. I watch him curiously as he pulls open the large steel door, gesturing for me to enter.

The moment the door latches closed I find it near impossible to see anything and my eyes have trouble adjusting from the bright sun outside to the dim interior.

Decklan once again takes my hand, pulling me towards the far wall of what appears to be a large open space. Nothing really comes into view until he flips on a light, and the entire room comes to life in an instant.

I gasp, my mind still trying to process what exactly it's seeing. Paintings, sculptors, sketches; there is art everywhere. Every wall and empty space of the room is lined with them, stretching from floor to ceiling, tucked in corners; it's like a book lover walking into the most exquisite library they could ever imagine. The view in front of me is absolutely breathtaking.

"Decklan." I barely manage to speak his name, my eyes tracing every inch of the large room.

It appears as though this room is the only room, the entire building opened up into one incredible space.

"What is this place?" I finally glance in his direction to find him studying my reaction.

"The S. Hartley Art Gallery," he says. "This is where Tim Porter brought Rosie on their first date." A smile spreads across his face.

"But how?" I start, remembering the dinner at the Porters when Gavin's mom told me the story.

"Tim frequented this gallery for years, bringing Rosie back here every year for their anniversary. The original owner of this gallery passed away just six months after Tim. At the funeral, his daughter gave Rosie a key, said she knew how much the gallery had meant to Tim and she wanted Rosie to be able to visit anytime she wanted. I may have asked to borrow that key," he tacks on, his grin deepening.

"I don't know what to say." I turn, slowly making my way to the far left wall. There's everything here; abstract, surrealism, expressionism. Each one is more beautiful than the one before it.

"Do you like it?" Decklan finally speaks after a long moment.

"Are you kidding?" I spin to find him standing directly next to me. "It's incredible. All of it." I gesture around the room.

"Rosie said most of the pieces here aren't worth much; painted by students, freelance artists, people whose names that you would likely not recognize."

"But that's what makes it so brilliant," I interject. "The most beautiful pieces are created by an artist who paints for themselves and not for money." I turn, continuing into the room.

It's not lost on me the magnitude of this moment. I find it hard to believe that Decklan would do something so personal, so incredible, for just anyone. The thought leaves me with a tight feeling in the pit of my stomach and makes it damn near difficult to breathe.

Glancing to my right, I catch sight of him, his gaze turned upward as he studies a rather devastating piece in front of him. It's of man, his hands stretched outward as if reaching for something he can't grasp. Dark clouds swirl through the background, the pain so apparent on the man's face it's almost like looking at a live photograph. His emotion seems to jump off the page at you.

"Amazing isn't it?" I step up next to him, entwining my fingers with his.

"I don't know much about art." He shrugs, his eyes not leaving the piece in front of him.

"You don't have to know much about art to feel the emotion the artist is trying to portray." I squeeze his hand, pulling his attention to me. "Thank you for this." My words are barely above a whisper. "Truly."

"You're welcome." The corner of his mouth pulls up in a slow smile just moments before his lips meet mine, the kiss slow and lingering.

The contact causes my insides to burn; my body coming to life under his touch, his kiss. It's at this moment that the truth becomes undeniably clear. I love him. It's sudden and powerful and scares me to my core, but I can't resist it. No matter how badly I want to...

**★★★★**

"You okay?" Decklan nudges my shoulder with his as we make our way from the small diner where he took me to dinner after leaving the art gallery.

"I am." I smile up at him, taking his hand when he offers it.

"You've been quieter than usual," he observes.

I hadn't really realized this fact until now. I guess I've just been so preoccupied with my realization earlier this evening that I didn't even notice. All I can think about is where I go from here, my future, what it would look like with Decklan or worse, without him.

"Sorry. Just tired I guess." I give him a sweet smile. "I've been in the lab for the last three nights trying to finish my final project of the semester. It doesn't help that Harlee wakes me up at the crack of dawn every morning either. I think I just need to sleep for like two days straight." My excuse is not completely untrue.

"You could always stay with me for a couple of days." He raises his eyebrows suggestively.

"Yeah, because I'm sure I would get tons of sleep that way." I laugh, shaking my head.

"What are you saying?" He fakes offense, his laughter abruptly cutting off as he stills beside me, his grip on my hand tightening.

"What..." My words fall off before I have a chance to finish, my eyes following Decklan's gaze to the man and woman exiting the restaurant just up ahead to our right.

I recognize him the moment his face comes into view. Trey.

It's clear to see he's spotted Decklan as well, veering in our direction almost instantly.

"Well, well, if it isn't my little brother." Trey steps directly in front of Decklan on the sidewalk, a lengthy brunette attached to his arm, the pair all but blocking our path. "Had I known you were in town I would have invited you to join us."

"Somehow I doubt that." Decklan's voice is tight, his gaze narrowed.

"You're probably right," he sneers. "You'd likely drink the bar dry and then take home a waitress or two. Oh, wait." His gaze turns to me, and I spot the recognition that crosses his features almost instantly. "You already found your waitress for the night it would seem." His eyes dart between the two of us.

"Trey Taylor." He extends his hand to me. "I believe we met a few weeks ago."

"Kimber." I force my voice even.

Taking his hand, I shake it lightly before pulling away. For whatever reason Decklan is not a fan of his brother, which means neither am I. I don't even have to question it. I don't know what the deal is with these two but regardless my loyalty stands firmly on this side.

"Kimber," he repeats back. "This is Anita, my fiancée." He introduces the brunette on his arm.

"Fiancée?" Decklan doesn't try to hide the surprise in his voice.

"Yes, well perhaps this wouldn't come as a shock to you if you actually called your family once in a while. How long has it been since you've spoken to Mom?" I can feel the judgment bleeding from every word he speaks.

"That's not any of your fucking business." Decklan seethes, clearly trying to contain the anger I can see starting to boil slowly below the surface.

"Actually, it is my business," Trey

protests. "She's my mother too, and if you think I'm going to just stand by and not say a word while you break her heart all over again, you're dead wrong."

"No one is breaking her heart." Decklan tries to act unaffected by his brother's comment but I can see it carries more weight than he'd likely admit.

"Is it not enough that she lost Conner?" Trey spits.

My mind immediately tries to piece together what they're talking about, but I can't ever remember him mentioning anyone by that name.

"Don't you fucking dare," Decklan threatens, his grip on my hand falling away.

"Don't I dare what, speak the truth? Just because you don't want to admit it to yourself, doesn't make it any less true. I tried to tell Mom to let you go, that she was better off without you, but do you think she listens to me? All she wants is for you to be in her life, and you can't even give her that. Not even after you..."

"Don't say it. Don't you even fucking think about it." Decklan's voice cuts through the air like ice, his tone causing a chill to run down my spine as I watch him stare daggers at his brother.

"Why not?" Trey throws his hands up, despite his fiancée's attempt to get him to walk away. "You ruin everything. You always have. But fuck if anyone says anything to Decklan. Fuck you. I won't walk on eggshells because it hurts you to admit what you did to Conner, what you did to all of us."

I can't even process the statement before I see Decklan swing, his fist connecting with Trey's jaw on a splintering crack. Trey stumbles backward, Anita immediately going to his aid. It takes him a few seconds to recover but when he finally straightens his posture and wipes the blood from his mouth, his focus goes to me not Decklan.

"I don't know what he's told you or who you think he is but if you want my advice, get out now. You have no idea what this asshole is capable of. I promise you, it won't end well for you." His words send my frantic heart pounding violently beneath my ribs.

A part of me wants to defend Decklan, to tell Trey he doesn't know what he's talking about, but I think deep down a part of me believes his statement. A part of me believes that this will end and when it does, I'll be the only casualty.

"Come on." Trey drops his arm around Anita, throwing one more vicious look towards Decklan before spinning around and walking away.

It takes me a few seconds to shake off the shock of what just happened before I finally turn my attention to Decklan. His eyes are fixed on Trey who is now several yards ahead, the look on his face enough to scare even me a little.

"Decklan," I say softly, gently resting my hand on his forearm.

He jerks away the moment the contact is made, spinning around to pin his wild eyes on me.

"Didn't you hear him?" he spits, stepping backward. "You need to stay away from me, Kimber."

"Don't do that," I get out weakly.

"Don't do what, admit he's right?"

"Don't push me away." I hate how desperate my voice sounds.

"Why not? You heard my brother. I'll only end up hurting you."

"I don't believe that," I object.

"Well believe it, Kimber, because every fucking word he said is the truth. I fucking destroy everything, everyone who gets close to me."

"You're only saying that because you're upset." I try to keep my voice calm, knowing if I get angry it will only further worsen the situation.

"I'm saying it because it's the fucking truth." His words tear through the air, their intensity causing me to take a step back.

"Fuck, Kimber." He sighs, his voice

dying down to just above a whisper as if he's admitting defeat. "Go home." He meets my gaze with a pained expression. "Just go home." He turns without another word and walks away, leaving me standing in the middle of the sidewalk.

I watch as he gets further and further away, torn between whether or not I should go after him or leave him be. I've never seen him upset, and to say I know how he would react if I went after him is far from true.

It isn't until he has completely disappeared from view that the reality of the situation seems to kick in. Spinning, I take off in the direction of the parking lot where his bike is, praying I can get there before he leaves.

It doesn't matter what Trey said or even what Decklan said for that matter. I know him. Deep down I do. And I know he would never intentionally hurt me.

Tonight was proof that there's so much more to Decklan than he lets people see. Behind his bad boy persona, the booze, motorcycles, and women, lies a man that *wants* more. I just don't think he knows how to be that man just yet.

No matter what caused this rift between the two brothers, no matter the past, I'm not giving up on Decklan. He may be willing to just walk away without a fight, but I'm not so

easily deterred from what I want.
*And right now all I want is him.*

# Chapter Seventeen

## **Decklan**

The nearly two-hour drive back to Portland does nothing to calm the anger that has been boiling inside of me since my confrontation with Trey. His words, the way he looked at me, you'd think I'd be used to it after all these years but time hasn't lessened the effect his hatred has on me.

It's one thing to hate myself. It's another thing entirely to have my only remaining sibling, someone I was extremely close to for most of my childhood, look at me with such disgust.

Then there's Kimber.

I feel like such an asshole for just leaving

her like that. She has nothing to do with any of
this, yet I punished her as if she were
somehow to blame.

I drop my helmet just inside the back
door and immediately head for the bar.
There's only one thing I want right now and
that's to wash away tonight's events with a
nice bottle of whiskey.

Thankfully the bar is pretty dead. The
last thing I want to do is deal with fucking
people right now. Sliding into a barstool at the
end of the bar, I signal Matt who appears in
front of me within moments, a glass in one
hand and a bottle of whiskey in the other. He
knows me well.

"You look like shit," he observes, filling
the glass to the rim before sliding it towards
me. "Rough night?"

"You could say that," I grind out,
draining the liquid in one long gulp. "And no,
I don't want to talk about it."

"Didn't think you did," he interjects.

Leaning forward, I snag the bottle of
whiskey from his hand, gesturing for him to
go. "I'm good here," I say, refilling the glass in
front of me.

Matt gives me a stiff nod before turning
and walking away.

Emptying the contents of the glass once
more, the familiar burn finds its way into the
pit of my stomach. It seems to settle nicely

there between my anger and regret.

****

"Decklan." A faint familiar voice breaks into my fog. "Decklan." The voice gets louder.

Lifting my head slowly from the bar, I spot Gavin just seconds before he slides down into the barstool next to me. It takes a moment for his face to come completely into view. I blink rapidly trying to clear my blurry vision.

"What the fuck man?" He seems irritated though I'm not sure I understand why he would be. Tack it onto the list I guess.

"What?" My voice catches in my throat just as a sharp pain shoots through my temple causing me to groan in discomfort.

"What the fuck are you doing here?" His question prompts me to look around at the brightly lit empty bar around me. "It's nine o'clock in the morning." He answers my question without me having to ask it. "Matt text me and said he left you here. Apparently he tried to get you to go upstairs, and you gave him a fat lip for his efforts."

"Fuck." I sigh, trying to piece together even a semblance of what happened last night.

"What's going on, Deck?" His tone falls serious.

"Nothing." I sway slightly when I

attempt to stand.

"Don't fucking lie to me, dude. I've known you for far too long. Getting so drunk you punch one of our employees and then pass out with your head down on the bar is not your style. So try again." He swivels his stool to face me when I finally manage to successfully plant both of my feet on the ground and push up into a stand.

"Did something happen with Kimber?" he asks.

For some reason his question sends anger rushing through me, seeming to pull me from my haze.

"Why would Kimber have anything to do with this?" I spit, my hard gaze focused directly on Gavin.

"Because my mom said you stopped by and picked up the key to the gallery; I just assumed you were taking her there."

"I did," I admit, not offering up any more information.

Truth is I am still trying to sort through what happened myself, my mind still tainted by the traces of last night's whiskey.

"And what happened?" He pushes for more.

"Nothing fucking happened. I took her to the gallery, I came home."

"And proceeded to drown yourself with almost an entire bottle of whiskey?" he questions, narrowing his gaze at me. "Why don't you tell me what really happened and stop acting like a pussy?"

"Fuck you, Gavin. I don't have time for this bullshit." I turn, sliding behind the bar to get a glass of water, my throat feeling like I spent last night drinking battery acid.

Taking a long drink, the cold crisp liquid seems to clear my head slightly, and I go in for another drink before I finally speak again, my gaze turned downward instead of at Gavin.

"We ran into Trey." I take another long drink before depositing the empty glass into the sink. "I think that about sums it up." I finally turn towards Gavin whose features have relaxed; understanding clear on his face.

"And what did big brother have to say this time?" He leans back, crossing his arms in front of his chest.

"The usual." I know I don't need to give him any more detail. He already knows the sort of shit Trey spews at me every time he has the misfortune of seeing me. "Only this time I took a shot at him. I think he will reconsider next time he wants to shoot off that fucking mouth of his."

"You hit him?" Gavin seems surprised, knowing how much shit I have taken from Trey in the past and not once having put my hands on him before.

As much as I loathe Trey and everything

he claims to stand for, at the end of the day he's still my brother and the only one I have left. As good as it felt to finally just lay his ass out, it felt equally as bad.

"He was running his fucking mouth in front of Kimber. I don't need her being drug into my bullshit. Besides, it's my business. He has no right spewing that shit in front of whoever the fuck he feels like."

"So did you tell her then? I mean, she must have had some questions."

"Fuck no." I shake my head adamantly. "Why would I?"

"Well she is your girlfriend, isn't she? Isn't that the kind of thing you share with someone you're dating?"

"We're not fucking dating." My tone goes hard. "Besides, after last night, I doubt she'll ever want to see me again."

"Why is that?" He arches an eyebrow at me.

"Because I told her to stay away from me and then proceeded to leave her stranded a good thirty-minute walk from her dorm." My stomach twists tightly at the thought of her walking that distance by herself after dark, probably confused as hell.

"What? Why the fuck would you do that?" Gavin pushes against the bar.

"Because it's what I needed to do."

"What the fuck does that mean?" he

spits, clearly pissed off at me though I'm not entirely sure why.

"I'm not good for her Gavin. She deserves better than what I can give her." The truth rips from my throat and seems to settle over us like a heavy weighted fog.

"Why do you do that? Why do you let Trey get into your fucking head and convince you that you aren't deserving of happiness?" He finally speaks after several long moments of silence.

"Because I don't deserve to be happy. Don't you get that? I fucking ruin everything."

"You choose to ruin everything. No one is standing in your fucking way but you. Fuck, Deck. Get your fucking head out of your ass and look around. That girl is changing you, in ways even I didn't think possible. And now, just like you always do, you're going to fuck that up too and then spend the next however many years blaming your past on why you can't be happy now. Conner is dead, Decklan, you're not," he spits, pushing out of his stool.

"Don't you fucking talk about Conner," I warn, pointing my finger in his direction.

"What are you going to do about it, Deck? Punch me, too? Bring it on. If that's what you need to do to fucking move past this shit, then do it. You think we all didn't lose something in that accident? Everyone loved Conner, you know that. And he wouldn't want this for you, you know that, too. He died and you lived, don't fucking waste that."

"Careful," I warn, feeling the control of my anger starting to slip.

"Fuck you," he snarls. "I'm your fucking best friend, Deck, hell I'm your brother. It's my duty to tell you when you're being a fucking prick, and right now you're really starting to grate on me. I get that you're hurting and that shit has been rough for you, I've been there through it all. Remember? But that doesn't mean I am going to just sit back and watch you self-destruct over your own damn bullheadedness. You have a chance to be happy, dude, to build a life. Why are you so hell bent on fucking that up?"

"I think you're putting too much stock into one girl," I object, though deep down even I can't deny the hold that one girl has on me.

"Am I?" He cocks his head to the side. "In the past few weeks, I have seen you act and do things I never thought you would. For the first time since Conner's death, I've seen you happy, and I mean fucking happy, Deck. Don't shit on that."

"What now, you're a fucking expert on happiness?" I let out a gruff laugh, somewhat amused by the thought.

"No, but I am an expert on your pansy ass." He smiles, the tension in the air all but vanishing in the matter of a few short seconds.

"Now do me a favor and call that fucking girl. I think you might owe her an apology."

"I don't know. I think I might have put a nail in that coffin," I admit, finding it hard to believe she would ever want to see me again after the way I acted last night.

"Well there's only one way to find out," he interjects. "Now, if you're just about done wallowing in your own self-pity, you may want to consider going upstairs and washing away last night's bottle. You look like shit."

"You're just pissed that even after the night I had I'm still better looking than you." I tilt my head back on a laugh.

"Fuck you." He laughs, stepping away from the bar. "I've got a few errands to run this morning. You good?"

"I'll live." I nod, gesturing for him to go.

"Call Kimber," he says, turning back to me just as he pulls the front door open.

"We'll see." I make no promises, laughing when he rolls his eyes and disappears into the morning sun.

Running my hands through my hair, I look around the bar trying to remember what the hell happened here last night. I have no recollection of punching Matt, which surprisingly I don't feel that bad for, nor do I have any fucking clue how I managed to sleep all night on a stool with the glass bar as my pillow.

I must have had a lot more to drink than I fucking realized...

I replay the confrontation with Trey in my mind as I climb the stairs and push my way inside my apartment. I don't know why after all this time I still let him get under my skin. I've heard the same shit from him for the last eight years now, yet it still has the same effect on me as it did back then.

Then there's Kimber. I can't shake away the look of desperation on her face as she begged me not to push her away. The fucking image seems to be burned into the back of my eyes.

Trey was right to warn her. She really should stay away from me. I know myself and I know there is no way I won't hurt her, but fuck me I just can't seem to let her go that easily.

It's easy to walk away in the heat of the moment, swearing you're doing it for the right reasons. But when the darkness of the night fades and you're faced with the reality of what you stand to lose, things aren't always so crystal clear.

On one hand, I want to do right by her. And I know the only way I can do that is to let her go. On the other hand, I want to be the selfish asshole I've always been and take exactly what I want until I no longer want it.

My head and heart have never been so

conflicted. The fact that I even have to think about it tells me that my feelings for this girl run a lot deeper than I'm ready to admit.

Am I really so convinced that I will hurt her or is my underlying fear that she will actually be the one to hurt me?

# Chapter Eighteen

## **Kimber**

Raising my fist to the door, I knock several times, the impact causing the wood to vibrate against my hand each time it connects. I know he's here, so I don't give up when he doesn't answer right away.

Letting out a frustrated sigh, I prepare to knock again but then stop with my hand in mid-air when the door jerks open. I'm greeted by the dark gaze of Decklan who is now standing directly in front of me still damp from the shower, a towel hanging loosely on his hips.

My mind goes blank for a long second, the drops of water sliding down his incredible torso enough to render me completely captive. It isn't until he speaks that the fog seems to lift and my resolve slips back into place.

"Kimber?" He seems surprised by my unannounced arrival.

"Good to see you're still alive," I snip, pushing my way past him without waiting for an invitation.

"What's that supposed to mean?" he asks, closing the door before turning to face me.

"Well, surely your cell phone must be broken. I mean, what other excuse would you have for abandoning me the way you did and then not even having the courtesy to answer the phone when I call just to make sure you got home okay." I ramble, unable to hide my anger over this whole situation.

I stewed all night about how to handle this before finally deciding that I would never be able to live with myself if I didn't at least put myself out there and fight for what I want. Sure, I'm upset, angry, hurt, disappointed, but that doesn't change the way I feel about Decklan, and I'm not prepared to let him go that easily.

He opens his mouth to speak, but I don't give him the chance to make any excuses.

"Don't," I shake my head. "I had a lot of time to think on my walk home last night." I narrow my eyes at him. "And you're gonna listen to what I have to say whether you like it or not. You owe me that much."

"The floor is yours." The crooked smile that pulls up one side of his mouth makes it damn near impossible for me to not crumble right here on the spot, but I refuse to let him distract me.

"First, do not ever walk away from me like that again. Ever. I get that there is a lot I don't know or understand about the relationship with your brother, but that gives you no right to take it out on me. Relationships are about being there for the other person. Friendships, marriages, that's all they are. What kind of relationship is this if at every turn you are shutting me out?"

I pause, gauging his reaction which remains unreadable.

"Second, you don't get to decide for me. If I choose to be with you, and I accept the risks that choice entails, then who are you to tell me otherwise? You decide for you, not me. If you don't want this..." I gesture between the two of us. "If you don't want me, then at least have the courage to say that and not try to play some martyr who is sacrificing himself for the girl."

"Look, I knew what I was getting into when I met you," I continue. "You never lied to me about what this is, or about what I should expect from this. And I haven't pushed you for more. You told me what you were capable of, and I accepted that knowing it probably wouldn't last. But now..." Emotion clogs my throat. "Now things have changed." I take a deep inhale and let it out slowly. "I no longer accept the original terms. I want more, Decklan, so much more. And if you tell me right now that you don't, at least I can walk away knowing I put myself out there and fought for what I wanted. But not saying anything at all would leave me with a life overflowing with regret, and I can't live that way. I know this is unfair, and I shouldn't demand things from you that you aren't capable of giving me, but that doesn't make me want them any less."

"Kimber." My name is weak on his lips.

"Please let me finish. I need to get this out before I lose my nerve." I stop him, meeting his deep gray gaze.

He gives me a brief nod, making no attempt to say more.

"I've never met anyone like you before. You're challenging, stubborn, and infuriating but also the most incredible person I have ever known. You have these moments where I swear you let me see you, really see you, for the man you are and not the man you let everyone believe you to be. I know you carry around a lot of pain and guilt. I may not know why, but it's clear to anyone who actually takes the time to pay attention that it's there. And I know that it's eating you alive, and if you don't find a way to deal with whatever it is, it will eventually consume you and then that man, the man I have come love, will surely disappear."

I see the surprise on his face, the way his eyes narrow in on mine at my words.

"I'm in love with you, Decklan. I don't how it happened or when, but I can't fight it. I love you, and I want to be with you. And not just a casual hookup, I want us to be together; really together. I want to help you with whatever it is you're fighting. I want you to know you're not alone and that you have someone on your side." I take a hesitant step towards him and then another, closing the gap between us to just a couple of feet.

"I'm sorry if this is not what you want to hear. And I'm sorry to just show up and lay all this on you at once. But I love you, Decklan, and I won't apologize for that. But I also understand if you don't feel the same, and if that's the case I will walk away and never bother you again. You have my word." I fight back the thickness that forms at the base of my throat at the thought. "I want you, Decklan. I choose you. Baggage and all."

"And what do I get?" His features remain tight as he finally speaks, but there is a hint of playfulness to his tone.

"Me," I get out weakly on a shrug.

I don't have time to say more before Decklan is stalking towards me, his lips crashing down on mine silencing what I planned to say next. Those words, along with all other coherent thoughts, simply float into nothingness as Decklan's mouth works skillfully against mine, kissing me so deeply and with so much hunger that it takes everything I have not to cower under his clear need for me.

"I'm sorry." He breathes against my lips, letting his towel fall away as he backs me towards the large circular support beam that stands in the center of the room.

"I don't deserve you." He pulls back to slide my shirt over my head, his eyes heatedly taking in my bare torso. "Fuck me." He dips his face, his lips finding the sensitive flesh just below my ear as his hands work effortlessly to free me of my pants.

Only moments pass before I feel the cool stone of the beam against my back as Decklan lifts me, pinning me between it and him.

"I want to feel you bare." He groans, sucking my bottom lip into his mouth.

"Then do it," I challenge, pulling back to meet his heated gaze.

I've never had sex without a condom before and the thought of feeling Decklan inside of me with no barrier is too much for me to resist. I've been on birth control since I was seventeen so I know we'll be okay, even if I was put on it for regulating my periods rather than to prevent pregnancy.

"What?" He hits me with surprised eyes.

"I'm on birth control." I place my hands on both sides of his face and pull his lips back to mine, feeling him smile against my mouth.

"Tell me again." He groans as he slides deeply inside of me, my legs locking tightly around his waist as he does.

"Tell you what?" I pant, my body suddenly so overcome by the thought and feeling of him inside me with nothing between us.

"That you love me." He pants, working into a slow steady rhythm.

My hands still at the back of his head, forcing his face up to meet mine.

"I love you." My words are breathy, the pleasure now coursing through every inch of my body nearly impossible to contain. "I love you, Decklan." I lean down, panting the words against his lips as he slowly increases his speed.

"Fuck. You feel so good around me." He groans out, taking my mouth on a hard heated kiss as his once controlled movements become more frantic and rapid, our bodies clashing together with so much force it takes everything I have to hold my grip around him.

"Decklan," I cry out, feeling the familiar warmth spread through my lower belly as he pounds relentlessly into me.

"Let it go, baby. Let me feel you." His words send my climbing pleasure over the edge, the waves cascading through my entire body as I tremble uncontrollably around him.

"That's it. Oh Fuck," he grinds out just seconds before I feel his release spill inside of me. The warmth of it spreads, the feeling unlike anything I've ever experienced before.

I drop my head onto Decklan's shoulder, unable to contain the smile on my face. I know there are risks with having unprotected sex, but I trust Decklan, as naive as that sounds, and I can't imagine another person I would want to share this experience with.

"Did I hurt you?" He stills inside of me, his face dropping into the crook of my neck.

"No," I get out weakly, still trying to catch my breath.

"You're incredible, you know that?" He pulls back, hitting me with a wide smile.

"So is that a yes?" I ask, leaning forward to lay a brief kiss to his lips.

"To more?" he questions, his gaze softening.

"To more," I confirm.

"I can't promise you that things will turn out the way you want, Kimber," he starts, my stomach knotting tightly at his words. "But I promise you there is nothing I want more in this world than you." His smile widens when he sees the relief that must be clearly written all over my face.

"Does this mean I get to call you my boyfriend?" I say jokingly, laughing when he curls his nose up playfully.

"If I get to have you like this anytime I want." He grinds against me, his erection still firmly inside of me. "Then you can call me anything you want." He smiles, pressing his lips once again to mine.

****

"So you have no siblings?" Decklan runs his fingers gently through my hair as I lay with my head propped on his firm chest.

The sound of his heart thumps loudly against my ear and is probably one of the most incredible sounds in the world.

"None," I confirm. "I don't think my parents' ever really wanted children. I'm pretty sure I'm the one and only mistake they ever made."

"Anyone who views you as a mistake is seriously fucking damaged." He laughs, his chest vibrating lightly beneath my cheek.

"I guess." I sigh. "I think having a child was just something to make them seem more wholesome. My father is in politics. He was the Mayor of the town I grew up in for years before running for State Senate. Mom is his doting perfect wife with her perfect little friends who sit around drinking tea and organizing fundraisers, criticizing the way other people live. It's pathetic."

"Do I sense some hostility?"

"You sense more than just hostility." I let out an exasperated laugh. "I love my parents', don't get me wrong, I just wish they trusted me enough to support my choices. They can't accept things that don't fit into their perfect idea of life. I don't even know why they're still together. My father clearly only keeps my mom around because she plays the role so well. I feel sorry for them honestly."

"Don't," Decklan whispers, dropping a kiss on the top of my head. "Don't even give them that. They don't deserve it. I understand you not wanting to cut them out of your life completely, but I think you're right to keep them at a distance until they come around. You shouldn't have to feel guilty about pursuing your dreams instead of someone else's."

"Thank you," I manage to get out, his comment meaning more to me than he probably realizes. "So what about your parents?" I ask, desperate to change the depressing topic that is my family life.

"Well you've met my mom," he says, my

mind immediately going back to the second time I ever saw Decklan, when he joined his mom and brother for lunch at the diner I work at.

"I didn't really know my father very well," he continues. "He skipped out on my mom when I was eight, and I haven't seen or spoken to him since."

"That's awful." I've never understood how someone could just leave their children like that, and the thought breaks my heart a little for Decklan.

"It was probably for the best." I feel him shrug beneath me. "Besides, my mom seemed happier without him."

"Tell me about your mom, what's she like?" I push for more, not sure if he will comply or not.

"Well, she's stubborn and bullheaded." He laughs.

"The apple doesn't fall far from the tree," I interject, laughing when he playfully squeezes my side.

"She also has a heart five times the size of a normal person. She cares very deeply for people in general, and she loves fiercely, especially her family." His voice trails off.

"Are you two close?"

"We used to be."

"What happened?" I can't help but ask.

"We just... I don't know, things just

happened and I ended up moving out my
senior year of high school."

"Is that when you stayed at the Porters?"
I don't balk at the vague answer he gives me,
clearly able to see it's not something he wants
to talk about right now.

"Yes," he confirms. "Rosie and Tim
always treated me like their second son. Hell,
before I officially lived with them I practically
lived with them already. They did more for me
than I think any of them ever realized." He
falls silent for a long moment.

"It must be nice, having a friend like
Gavin." I finally speak again.

"It is," he agrees. "Though sometimes I'd
like to run him over with my motorcycle." He
laughs.

"I wish I had friends like that."

"Well, first you'd have to buy a
motorcycle." He jokes prompting me to lay a
swift smack to the top of his thigh.

"Shut up." I laugh.

"Surely you had friends you were close
to growing up." He falls serious again.

"Not really, no. I was too busy with my
advanced classes, student council, piano and
cello lessons, to really have time to devote to
friends. I mean I had friends, just not the kind
that stayed in touch after I moved to Oregon."
I shrug.

"What about your roommate; you two

seem close?"

"Harlee?" I question. "I mean, yeah I guess. I'm certainly closer to her than I ever was any of my friends back home. I got so lucky when I landed her as my roommate. Not many people could live with me."

"I don't know. I think I could." He laughs, shifting his body causing me to roll onto my back. Within moments he's on top of me, settling between my thighs.

"I wonder why." I reach between us, my fingers closing down around his already hard erection. "That's what I thought." I smile knowingly, tightening my grip.

"That's not the only reason." He smiles down at me. "You also make one hell of a sleeping partner." He grinds into my hand.

"I do?" I question playfully, confused by his statement.

"You really do," he confirms. "You barely move or make any sound at all. I had to check your breathing twice last night out of fear that I somehow fucked you to death."

"As if that is possible." I can't contain the laughter that bursts from my throat.

"If it were I think we would have accomplished it by now," he agrees, a wide smile on his impossibly handsome face.

"We could always try harder." I give him a heated look as I position the tip of his erection at my entrance.

"Challenge accepted." He groans, sliding deeply inside of me.

# Chapter Nineteen

**<u>Decklan</u>**

"Good morning." I drop a kiss on Kimber's forehead when she opens her eyes and peers up at me sleepily.

"Morning." She smiles. "What time is it?"

"Just after nine." I push her wild hair away from her face.

"That early?" she questions. "I feel like I could sleep for at least ten more hours." She groans, rolling onto her side away from me, bunching the blanket up around her head.

"We could do that." I pull her backside flush with my body, dropping my face into the crook of her neck. "Or we could go get something to eat." I kiss her soft skin, loving the way goosebumps spread across her flesh when I do.

"Oh my God, food." She groans. "I feel like I haven't eaten in days."

"Well considering we've been holed up here for two days with nothing to eat but snack food, you kind of haven't." I laugh, kissing the bottom of her jaw. "What do you say we take a shower and then I take you to breakfast?"

"I say that sounds amazing." She smiles, turning in my arms as she pulls my face down to hers, her soft lips brushing gently against mine.

**\*\*\*\***

"What time do you guys open?" Kimber glances around as we make our way through the empty bar.

"Depends on the day." I clasp my hand around hers, pulling her through the front door behind me before turning to lock it. "Usually, through the week, we open at five. It really doesn't pay for us to keep it open through the day."

"That makes sense," she agrees, taking my hand again when I offer it. "So where we are we going?" she asks, snuggling into my side, the morning temperature cool and crisp.

"Well considering it's too cold to throw you on my bike, how about we just head over there for coffee and bagels?" I nod my head towards the coffee shop/bakery across the street.

"Oh my God, coffee sounds so good right now." She shakes her head excitedly, pulling a huge smile on my face.

My God, this fucking girl is too fucking beautiful for her own good. The way the light bounces off her blonde hair gives her a glow as she stands in the bright morning sun.

Fucking breathtaking.

Wrapping my arm around her shoulder, I kiss her temple before quickly leading her across the street. Holding the door open the moment we reach the front entrance, I usher her inside.

I hear Gavin's voice boom through the small space within seconds of the door latching closed behind us, pulling my attention to the only occupied table in the far corner of the room.

"He's alive." He laughs, grabbing the attention of Kimber as well.

It takes me a moment to realize he's not alone and even longer to recognize the guy sitting across from him.

"Paxton?" I don't try to hide the surprise in my voice. "What the hell, dude, I didn't know you were in town," I say, making my way towards their table, dragging Kimber along with me.

"It's good to see you, Deck." He stands, giving me a one-armed hug. "I actually got in yesterday. You didn't answer your phone so I had to stay with this asshat." He laughs, gesturing behind him to Gavin.

"Fuck you, dude," Gavin jokingly objects.

"And who is this beautiful creature," he asks, turning his attention to Kimber.

"That's the girl I was telling you about," Gavin interjects before I can answer, smiling widely at Kimber who sinks slightly beneath the gaze of all three of us.

"When Gavin told me a woman had finally reeled this one in, I didn't believe it," he says, smacking my shoulder. "I gotta say I see why now." He gives her a warm smile and extends his hand to her. "Paxton Stewart."

"Kimber James," she responds, reaching out to shake his hand.

"Well, it is very nice to meet you, Kimber James." He flicks his gaze towards me for a split second before focusing back on Kimber.

"You, too." She smiles, nervously tucking her hair behind her ear.

"Paxton is one of our friends from high school. He moved to California a couple of years ago," I explain to Kimber before turning back to Paxton. "How long are in town for?"

"Indefinitely." He smiles, running a hand through his dark hair.

Out of all of us, Paxton has always been the diva of the group, always making sure his facial hair is well trimmed, his hair perfectly styled, and he never fails to sport the latest 'in' look. It's good to see that some things never change.

"You're coming back?" I ask surprised, considering he hasn't mentioned anything about moving back over the last few times I've spoken to him.

"Yeah, it's time," he confirms.

Not wanting to push the issue at the current moment, I give him an understanding nod and leave it at that. Paxton has had a rough couple of years and if anyone understands that it's me.

"Gavin said you guys could give me a couple time slots at the bar until I can nail down something more permanent," he adds on.

"Of course," I agree. "Paxton plays one hell of an acoustic set," I explain to Kimber.

"Why don't you two join us?" Paxton interrupts, gesturing to the table where Gavin is still sitting.

"Let me grab us something to eat first." I snag Kimber's hand, giving it a firm squeeze.

"Of course, I can imagine you've worked up quite an appetite." Gavin laughs, raising his eyebrows suggestively at us.

"You're a dick." I shake my head, spinning around and walking towards the front counter with Kimber fast on my heels.

****

"So Paxton used to live here, why'd he leave?" Kimber asks, sliding her arm through mine as we finally exit the coffee shop an hour and a half later.

"His mom got sick," I explain.

"Is she better now, is that why he's back?"

"She actually died five months ago."

"That's awful." Kimber tightens her grip on my arm.

"It's good that he's back, though. This is home to him."

"So then he was friends with you and Gavin growing up?" she asks.

"More like family really. The three of us have been through a lot together."

"Can I ask you a question?" She peers up at me just as we stop at the front entrance of the bar. "Did you know Gavin slept with Harlee?" Her question catches me off guard.

"He did?" I question, finding it odd that he wouldn't tell me something like that if it actually happened.

"A couple of nights after the Halloween

party," she confirms.

"I had no idea," I answer honestly.

"She really likes him. Apparently the feelings aren't reciprocated. He's blown her off ever since."

"I don't involve myself in that aspect of his life, Kimber," I say, knowing that she's likely looking for an explanation.

"No, I know." She shakes her head. "I just wasn't sure if you knew about it."

"I didn't." I wrap my arms around her and pull her into my chest, dropping a kiss to the top of her head. "Do you really have to go home today?" I speak into her hair.

"I have to work this afternoon." She sighs.

"What about tomorrow?" I ask, not quite ready to let her go just yet.

"I have class until two and then I work the dinner shift." She pulls back, hitting me with a mischievous look. "But we still have a couple more hours before I have to head back." She raises her eyebrows suggestively.

"I like the way you think," I growl, dropping my mouth to hers.

\*\*\*\*

"What the fuck dude? Why didn't you tell me you fucking slept with Kimber's roommate?" I slide into a stool at the high top bar table where Paxton and Gavin are sitting having drinks.

"Well hello to you, too." He takes a long drink of his draft beer. "Where the fuck have you been?"

"I had to drive Kimber home. Now answer the fucking question."

"I don't tell you every girl I sleep with." He leans back, crossing his arms in front of his chest.

"Yes, you do actually." I shake my head. "You make it a point to make sure everyone knows."

"I do not." He fakes innocence, looking to Paxton for backup.

"Don't look at me." Paxton holds his hands up on a laugh. "If things are still the way they were when I left two years ago, which I'd say they are, then I'm only going to hurt your case."

"Whatever. Fuck you guys." Gavin slams back the rest of his beer in one drink. "I need another beer." He spins, storming off towards the bar.

"What's got his panties in a twist?" Paxton laughs, leaning forward to rest his elbows on the table.

"That's a very good question," I observe.

"So Kimber huh?" Paxton pulls the conversation to me. "I gotta say, dude, I didn't think you were capable of a relationship."

"Neither did I. I mean, it's still pretty new," I admit. "But this girl, I don't know, dude, she's different."

"I'm happy for you, man." He clasps my shoulder. "Truly."

"I appreciate that." I try to fight the smile that creeps across my face.

"Man, you've got it bad." He laughs, shaking his head at me.

"I do," I finally answer, not realizing how good it would feel to finally admit it out loud.

"How's everything else going? How's your mom?"

"She's good. I don't really see her that often, for obvious reasons, but she seems to be doing pretty well." I nod at Gavin when he reappears, sitting a glass of whiskey down in front of me.

"And Trey?" Paxton continues.

"Fucking dick hole," Gavin interjects.

"Boy things really haven't changed have they? I mean other than the fact that Deck has gone and got himself pussy-whipped." He winks, clearly just joking. "The anniversary of the accident is coming up soon isn't it?" The serious change of conversation causes my whole body to tense.

"Two weeks," I confirm, raising the glass to my lips.

I take a deep inhale before pouring the liquid into my mouth, the burn an instant relief from the panic and dread that has slowly started to creep its way into my throat.

"I'll have to stop out and visit the cemetery," he continues. "I can't believe it's been eight years." He shakes his head.

"It's crazy right?" Gavin tacks on. "Where has the time gone?"

"No doubt. Feels like just yesterday when we would hide out in Deck's basement and get stoned off our asses. Do you all remember how Trey used to always try to sneak down and bust us?" Paxton laughs.

"God even then he was a tool," Gavin agrees. "But you gotta admit we had some good times."

"That we did," Paxton confirms.

The guys continue to reminisce, reliving all the bullshit we used to pull as teenagers, but my mind is too preoccupied with the thought of what happened after all those memories to really enjoy the moment.

Sure we had some fucking killer times, but those vanished along with almost everything else in the matter of one night. One night changed my entire life and ended another's. No matter how much time passes, I don't think I'll ever be able to move past it.

The accident has defined who I am since the moment it happened. I tried to piece myself back together afterward but nothing ever felt the same. So instead of healing, I perfected my exterior; learned how to fake it so that no one had to suffer along with me. I had already caused enough pain, who was I to ask for relief?

But now there's Kimber; a bright light shining through my very dark tunnel. For the first time in eight years, I feel something beyond what I lost... I feel hope.

# Chapter Twenty

## **<u>Kimber</u>**

I swear I feel like class was never going to end today. This is the first time in four days that my schedule is clear enough that I can make the trip up to Portland tonight, and to say I'm excited is quite an understatement. I've been a bundle of anxious energy all day.

"Kimber?" I freeze just feet from the front steps of my dorm building the moment the familiar voice washes over me.

Turning slightly, the instant Garrett's face comes into view my stomach bottoms out.

"Garrett?" I question, confusion and shock clear in my voice. "What? What are you doing here?" I stutter over my words.

He gives me a hesitant smile and takes a step towards me.

"I'm sorry, Kim. When they said they were coming, I knew I had to come, too. I had to see you."

"They?" I question, my mind swirling. "My parents'? They're here? In Oregon?" Even as I ask the question, I already know the answer. I can tell by the look on his face that I am spot on.

"They want to see you." He takes another step towards me, his hand coming to a rest on my forearm.

"And what, you're their little messenger boy?" I jerk away from his touch, anger boiling in my throat.

"I'm here to help you, Kim."

"It's Kimber!" I grind out. "Shit." I step back, panic starting to set in.

"Shit. Shit. Shit." I run my hands through my hair, the thought of facing my parents' in person the last thing I want to deal with right now.

"Is that really necessary? People can hear you." Garrett looks around before meeting my gaze again.

"Do you think I care?" I snip.

"You should." His tone remains soft though I can tell by how tight his features are that it's forced.

"Well, I don't."

"Who are you?" He stares back at me like he's looking at a complete stranger.

I guess to him I kind of am. He's not used to this Kimber, the real Kimber.

"Where are they?" I ignore his comment, pinning my eyes directly on him.

"They're staying at the *Smithson Resort*. They were hoping you would agree to have dinner with them tonight."

"So you really are the messenger then?" I'm surprised that I'm shocked but in a small way, I kind of am. "What's in this for you?" I cock my head to the side.

"What's that supposed to mean?" His voice goes up a notch. "I'm here because I care about you."

"Bullshit." I ignore the way his eyes narrow with disapproval at my language.

"Kimber, be reasonable. I care about you, your parents' care about you. It's just dinner. It's the least you can do after they've come all this way."

"After they've come all this way without telling me you mean?"

"Please." His tone softens. "One dinner."

"Fine," I groan out, knowing there is no way I'm going to get out of this. If I refuse it's likely my father will be the next to show up, and that's the last thing I want.

"Perfect." He smiles. "We have reservations at *Watsons*. Your father will send a car for you. Seven o'clock sharp."

"Seven," I confirm, sighing loudly before spinning and walking away.

\*\*\*\*

"I'm sorry I had to cancel our plans." I sigh into the phone.

"It's okay," Decklan reassures me. "I think I can survive one more day."

"You think?" I laugh, adjusting the hem of my dark gray sheath dress.

"It might be more than I can take." His voice drops low. "I might just have to pay you a little unexpected visit. Seems to be the theme tonight."

"Yeah but the difference is your visit would be welcome."

"Would it now? Well in that case..." He laughs lightly.

"Don't make it worse," I whine. "It's bad enough that I don't get to see you, now I have to endure my parents' for the next few hours."

I purposely leave out the fact that Garrett is with them. I know it's wrong of me to omit this information, but I just don't have it in me to tell him that I will also be spending my evening with my ex-boyfriend who I dated for three years and is the only other man I've slept with. Besides, it's not like I would ever go there again, even if Decklan wasn't in the picture.

"Why go then?" he asks curiously, interrupting my inner battle.

"Because they're my parents'." I sigh. "I know things aren't great between us, but a small part of me really wants to salvage what little of our relationship remains."

"I get that. I'm sure everything will be fine," he reassures me. "Call me after."

"I will," I say, clicking off the phone before dropping it into my lap.

Looking out of the backseat of the town car my father sent to pick me up, I can't help but wonder how my parents' would react to me dating Decklan. Would they see the incredible man that I see or would they see only what they want to see; a man who lives in a bar, dresses in ripped jeans and leather, and drives a motorcycle?

I can't see them being very receptive to the idea, even if our relationship isn't as damaged as it currently is. The thought makes me sad. They would be so quick to judge him for being different than them, and he would never have a chance to show them who he really is.

"Ma'am." The driver pulls me from my fog and I look up to see we have arrived at the restaurant.

It's only seconds before Garrett is pulling open the door and helping me out of the car, sure to kiss my cheek the moment I step up next to him. I do my best not to cringe under his touch as I take the arm he offers and allow him to lead me inside.

My stomach is a ball of nerves as Garrett guides me through the restaurant. It's elegant and far too fancy for my personal taste which means my parents' probably absolutely love it. I guess none of the restaurants near campus were up to their standards which is why they chose a location over thirty minutes away.

I finally spot my parents', who are seated at a small intimate four-person table in the corner of the room. My mother sees me first, a tight smile forming on her thin lips as she stands.

She looks exactly as I remember: her dark blonde hair pulled back in a tight bun, a navy suit dress and blazer covering her small frame. It's strange how I'm just now noticing how much I look like my mother. We're the same build, same height, same eye and hair color. It's weird that I've never really noticed before.

"Kimber," she croons, pulling me into a weak hug like she's afraid to touch me.

"Mother." I step back and give her a soft smile before nodding towards my father.

He looks like he's aged five years in the four months I've been here; thick patches of gray hair pepper his temples and his eyes are lined with dark bags. He keeps his gaze firmly on me as I slide into the seat that Garrett pulls out for me directly across from him.

"Well it's good to see you're still dressing appropriately," he observes, unfolding his napkin as he lays it into his lap.

"I am capable of dressing myself." I try to keep the sarcasm from my voice, but it still seeps out thick and full of resentment.

Thankfully our waitress appears before anyone can say anymore. It isn't until several moments later after drinks are served and orders are taken that I find myself back in the spotlight of my parents' glare.

"So Garrett tells us the restaurant you're working at is nice." My mother speaks first, a desperate attempt to make small talk.

"It is," I confirm.

"If you came home you wouldn't have to work," My father immediately interjects. "You would be able to focus on your studies instead of wasting your time serving others."

"I like my job. You speak as though it's beneath me, and it's not. I am no more special than the next person."

"You are, too." His tone is low and warning. "You are my daughter."

"Biologically maybe," I agree. "But in the way that it counts, no I'm not."

"How dare you, after all we've done for you."

"Will you two stop?" My mother objects. "This isn't helping matters."

Garrett chimes in, distracting my father enough with talks of politics and re-election and we are at least able to make it through dinner without killing each other. It isn't until after the plates have been cleared away and the realization sets in that sooner or later we are going to have to talk that my mother finally turns the conversation back to me.

"Kimber, why don't you tell us about your studies?" she suggests. "How are classes going?"

It takes less than two minutes before my father is at it again. The moment I mention Art he's off on another rant, talking about how I'm wasting my time and that my degree will never amount to anything.

"Art is not an acceptable major; I've said this time and time again," he objects.

"Luckily it's not up to you to decide," I bite back.

"Is this the way we raised you?" The look of disgust on his face as he stares back at me tells me everything I need to know; this is never going to work.

"You're never going to accept me for who I am, are you?" I question, cocking my head to the side. "You're never going to stop trying to change me?"

"Not until I've talked some sense into

you; no," he answers without hesitation.

"Then we're done here." I stand, ignoring my mother's protests to sit back down.

Shoving away from the table, I am out of the restaurant and already several feet outside before Garrett's voice catches up to me.

"Kimber, wait." I hear him say just moments before his hand clasps down on my forearm, spinning me towards him.

"Get off of me, Garrett," I bite, shaking his hand away.

"Stop this. Come back inside," he demands.

"No." The anger in my voice is enough to derail Garrett's attempt at getting me to go back.

"Okay. Okay." He holds his hands up in front of himself. "At least, let me take you back to your dorm."

"I can find my own way." I insist, knowing the car that dropped me off is long gone and my only other option is to call a cab, which I will gladly do if it means getting me the hell out of here.

"Don't be ridiculous. Come on, I'll drop you off," he says, taking my elbow as he leads me towards the valet station.

As much as I don't want to sit in the car with Garrett for the next thirty minutes, I also know it's my quickest way out of here and right now that's all I want to do. I need to put as much space as I can between me and my father as quickly as possible.

It's only minutes before I am sitting in the passenger seat of Garrett's rental car, panic gripping at my chest as the reality of my situation sinks in. I've lost all hope of regaining any type of relationship with my parents'. There would be hope for my mother if not for my father. But she would never choose me over him, and he has clearly drawn that line. That's it, it's over. The thought of how completely alone I am in the world suddenly seems to settle over me like a thousand pounds of rubble, burying me beneath their weight.

Garrett tries to talk to me, but I'm too lost in my own thoughts to really process anything he's saying. After a couple of minutes, he eventually stops trying; the remainder of the car ride a silent one.

When he finally pulls up outside of my dorm room and slows to a stop, I am so eager to escape the confines of the car that I am ripping open the door before he even has the car in park. Slamming it behind me, I'm crossing the space towards my dorm building within seconds.

"Kimber, wait," he hollers after me, but I don't stop. I just need to get the hell away from all of this. "Kimber." His voice sounds directly behind me just moments before his hand closes down around my bicep, jerking me to a stop.

"Would you stop already?" he grinds out, spinning me to face him. "I know things didn't go as planned tonight, and I'm sorry about that." He releases my arm, his fingers gently gliding across the part he was just squeezing. "But I have something to say, and you need to hear it."

"Garrett don't," I start but he cuts me off.

"I'm still in love with you, Kimber, that hasn't changed."

"I'm sorry, I don't feel the same."

"Yes you do," he insists. "Look, you're rebelling right now and you know your parents' want us together, so that's the last thing you want to give them. But forget about them for a moment and think about me, about us. I know you miss the way we used to be."

"That's just it, Garrett, I don't. I'm sorry." I drop my tone, guilt creeping its way into the pit of my stomach.

"I don't believe that. You love me, Kimber. You know that as much as I do. You just need to remember how great we are together."

It seems like the seconds disappear between him closing in on me to the point where his lips meet mine. The moment the connection is made, I know it's wrong. Every single thing about it feels wrong.

"What are you doing?" I push at his chest.

"I'm reminding you." He dips his head again, only this time, I'm prepared and I turn my face to the side to avoid his kiss.

It isn't until I do, that I see him: Decklan. He's standing just a few yards away, close enough that I know he can see me under the well-lit dorm entrance but far enough away that I doubt he grasps what is actually taking place.

"Stop." I push Garrett as hard as I can before spinning towards Decklan.

I know the second I reach him what he's thinking. Betrayal and anger line his features as he turns away and stalks towards his bike which is parked just feet away.

"Decklan, wait." I finally reach him as he climbs onto his bike and slides his helmet on. "It's not what you think." I pant, trying to catch my breath.

"No?" He cocks his head to the side, his face hidden behind the visor of the helmet making it impossible to read his reaction. "Because to me it looks like you were making out with your ex-boyfriend who you just happened to forget to tell me was here." He fires the engine to life, drowning out my attempt to explain.

"Decklan, please," I yell over the noise, panic seizing my entire body as he backs out of the parking lot and speeds off on his bike without once looking in my direction again.

A sob tears through my chest and I kick at the ground, furious that I even put myself in this position to begin with. Spinning I stalk back towards Garrett who has not moved from the spot I left him in.

"Get out the hell out of here, Garrett." I seethe, stepping directly in front of him.

Without another word I rear back and swing, my hand connecting with his cheek on a loud smack that echoes through the night air.

"And do not ever come back here again." I ignore his expression of shock and confusion as I spin and quickly walk away.

# Chapter Twenty-one

## **<u>Kimber</u>**

"Decklan, it's Kimber. Please call me back. I can explain last night. I know what you're probably thinking, but I can assure you it's not at all what it probably looked like. Please." I sigh into the phone, not sure what else to say. "Just call me."

I press the end button and drop my phone onto the bed, rubbing my eyes with the back of my hands. I'm exhausted, drained. I got very little sleep last night having spent most of it trying to reach Decklan.

It's been nearly twenty-four hours and he hasn't answered even one of my calls or texts. I even get the run around when I call the bar. It's beyond frustrating. If I had my own car I would probably have already driven to Portland myself. I'm just not prepared to pay a cab to drive me all the way there just to have him refuse to see me, which I get the feeling is likely what would happen.

"No luck?" Harlee exits the bathroom, her wet hair knotted up in a large bath towel.

"None." I sigh. "I just don't get it. Why won't he at least give me the chance to explain?"

"Put yourself in his shoes, girl. How would you feel if you showed up at the bar to surprise him and saw him kissing his ex-girlfriend which he purposely didn't tell you was in town? Would you not think the worst?"

Even I can't argue with that logic. I know I need to just give him some time to cool off. But having him think the worst of me is eating me from the inside out. I *need* him to know the truth and not the version of truth he thinks is fact, but the actual truth.

"Just give it some time. Decklan is crazy about you, anyone can see that. He'll come around." She flips her head over, rubbing the towel through her long blonde hair to soak up any excess water left over from the shower.

"But what if he doesn't?" I meet her gaze when she straightens her posture, dropping the towel onto the back of the desk chair.

"He will," she reassures me. "Trust me, I

get how hard it is to just let things be. I'm experiencing a taste of that myself, but you can't force this. You can't make him listen to you if he's not ready to."

"Still no word from Gavin?" I gladly change the course of the conversation, picking up on her hidden meaning.

"Nope." She shakes her head, running her fingers through her tangled hair. "I don't think I will either. If he hasn't reached out to me by now, I don't think he will. I guess it was only a matter of time before someone gave me a taste of my own medicine." She gives me a sad smile.

"So where are you going tonight again?" I ask, having been in too much of a fog when she told me earlier to really retain the information.

"Woodfire Grill." She turns, grabbing the lotion from her nightstand. "I'd invite you but it's not really a group thing."

"You're going on a date?" I ask, honestly a little surprised considering she's been so hung up on Gavin these past couple of weeks.

"You remember Bryan?" she asks.

"The hot surfer guy from your English class?" I question, knowing exactly who she's referring to. He's only been following Harlee around like a lost puppy since the first week of classes.

"That's the one," she confirms. "Well, he

finally talked me into going to dinner with him."

"Good for you." I smile. "He's probably over the moon."

"He's a sweetheart and totally hot. I don't why I never really saw it before," she admits.

"Me either." I agree.

"Alright, I have to finish getting ready." She grabs her makeup bag from the top of the dresser. "You good?"

"I'm good," I lie, giving her a forced smile.

"Good." She nods, disappearing back into the bathroom.

\*\*\*\*

It's been almost a week...

A week and still no word from Decklan. I have stewed, imagined the worst, and even resorted to drowning myself in a bottle of wine with Harlee last night.

I've reached my breaking point.

Decklan is going to talk to me whether he likes it or not.

Pulling Angel's car into the lot behind *Deviants*, I kill the engine and slide out, my stomach knotted so tightly I feel like I might vomit at any moment. I don't know why I'm so nervous. Maybe because I know I'm not wanted here, or maybe it's because this is so completely out of character for me that I don't know how to reel myself in.

Walking around to the front entrance, I let out a deep sigh when the door opens with no resistance. Knowing they don't open for another fifteen minutes, I wasn't sure if it would be unlocked. Taking another deep inhale I step inside, temporarily blinded by the dimly lit bar that is a stark contrast to the late afternoon sun. Blinking rapidly, it takes several long seconds before my surroundings come into view.

I jump slightly when Val suddenly appears behind the counter, standing from her crouching position where she's likely stocking the coolers that sit beneath the bar.

"Kimber." She spots me instantly. "What are you doing here?" Her tone is casual which makes me think she has no idea about what's been going on which I use to my advantage.

"I was just stopping in to surprise Decklan, is he home?" I ask, stopping directly next to the bar.

"I don't know. I haven't seen him. But you're welcome to go check." She gestures to the door that leads up to Decklan's apartment. "If he's up there will you let him know I need him to call *Louie's*; they shorted us an entire case of top shelf."

"Sure." I smile, knowing it's probably the

last thing I will think of if I actually get to lay eyes on him.

"Thanks." She nods, turning her back to me as she continues prepping the bar.

Without another word I head up to Decklan's apartment, my heartbeat increasing with each step I climb, feeling like it might pound out of my chest by the time I reach the top. I stop directly in front of his door, not sure if I have the courage to knock.

I stare at the chipped wood for several long seconds before finally lifting my hand and rapping it gently against the door. I immediately hear footsteps as they cross the room, and my breath catches in my throat when I hear the lock click.

This is it.

There's no going back now.

Taking another deep inhale, I falter slightly when Paxton appears in front of me.

"Kimber." He makes no attempt to move out of the doorway or to invite me in. "It's really not a good time."

"Is he here?" I ignore his comment.

"He is, but you don't want to see him right now." His voice is gentle, but I can tell by the look on his face how serious he is.

"I think I'll be the judge of that," I say, stepping towards him, my attempts to get inside immediately thwarted when he stands firm in the doorway not allowing me to pass.

"Trust me on this one, Kimber," he warns. "He's in a rough way right now, and there's no reasoning with him when he gets like this."

"I appreciate the heads up; now move out of my way, Paxton." I stand my ground, prepared to stand here all day if that's what it takes to see Decklan.

"Okay." He steps back, holding his hands up. "But don't say I didn't warn you." He grabs his jacket from the hook next to the door and steps out of the apartment as I step inside. "Good luck. Who knows, maybe you can talk some sense into him," he says, disappearing down the stairs.

Confused by his cryptic warnings, I slowly close the door and turn to scan the apartment. I jump slightly when a loud bang sounds from the bathroom and the door flies open, a shirtless Decklan stumbling out, a nearly empty bottle of whiskey clutched in his fingers.

"Decklan?" His name falls from my lips as I take in his state.

The moment his eyes hit mine it's clear to see what Paxton was talking about. His natural messy hair is an unruly mess of tangles, his facial hair is bushier than normal, and his incredible gray eyes have lost a bit of their luster, dark circles now lining them. He's dressed only in a pair of jeans hanging loosely on his hips, his incredible toned body otherwise on full display.

"What the fuck?" he slurs, clearly drunk, his staggered movements giving that away before he even opened his mouth. "What are you doing here?" He stumbles towards the couch, collapsing onto it the moment he reaches it.

"You haven't returned any of my calls; I didn't really have any other choice," I say, not moving from my place just feet from the door.

"Perhaps that should have given you the hint." He lifts the bottle to his lips and takes a long gulp.

"Don't you think you've had enough?" I ask, crossing the space towards him, gesturing to the drink in his hand.

"I'll decide when I've had enough," he snaps, his tone harsher than I've ever heard before. "I still don't even know why the fuck you're here."

"Because I wanted to see you." I hesitantly take a seat on the ottoman just a few feet from him. "I needed to apologize."

"I don't want to hear it." He avoids my gaze, dropping his head onto the back of the couch as he stares up at the ceiling.

"Well you're going to hear it whether you like it or not," I bite, my frustration mounting. "Had you let me explain the other night, you would have known that Garrett pushed himself on me. I didn't even kiss him back. Hell, I was trying to get him off of me. The only reason I was even with Garrett was because I was so desperate to get away from my father. I'm sorry I didn't tell you he was in town, too. I see now how that looks, but you have to believe that I feel nothing for him. He's out of my life, for good this time."

"I don't care." He meets my gaze, his eyes dark.

"Really? You don't care? Is that why you're sitting here drowning yourself in a bottle of whiskey?" I lean forward, able to snag the bottle from his hand before he even has a chance to react.

"What the fuck, Kimber," he growls, struggling to get off the couch in time to stop me from dumping the remainder of the bottle into the sink.

He reaches me just as I slam the now empty container onto the counter.

"You realize I live above a bar right?" He grabs the bottle. "I'll just fucking get more."

He swings the bottle loosely between his fingers before throwing it forcefully across the room. It hits the far wall on a loud crash, the glass shattering against the exposed brick before scattering across the floor.

"Are you kidding me right now?" I gape at him.

"Do I fucking look like I'm kidding?" he challenges.

"Why are you doing this?" I drop my tone, tears welling behind my eyes.

"Because this is who I am." His words are a warning. "This is the real me. You like what you see? Is this what you want?" He steps up directly in front of me, his whiskey breath hot on my face.

"I want you, but not like this." I meet his gaze, my hands coming to rest on his bare chest.

"Well too bad," he growls.

"Is this really all about Garrett?" I call after him as he spins away from me.

"This has nothing to fucking do with your stupid fucking pussy ass ex-boyfriend."

"Then why are treating me like this?" I ask, hating how weak my voice sounds.

He stops in the middle of the living room and turns back towards me, his expression pained.

"Because I can't do this anymore."

"Why?" I plead for him to give me some sort of explanation.

"Don't you fucking get it?" His voice rips through the space of the room. "Seeing you with that asshole showed me that you have the power to hurt me."

"I'm sorry, that was never my intention," I start.

"It fucking hurt me because I'm in love with you." His words break in the middle as he lets out a defeated exhale.

"What?" I can feel the heat rush to my cheeks.

"I love you, Kimber, and I can't fucking love you." His words feel more like an apology than a confession.

"I don't understand." I take a couple steps towards him, but he steps away when I get too close.

"I'm a fucking tornado, Kimber. I will rip through your life and destroy every single thing you love."

"I don't believe that." I shake my head.

"Believe it," he warns. "I always hurt the people who are closest to me the most. I could never forgive myself for hurting you."

"But you are hurting me," I plead, wiping away a tear that escapes my eye.

"It's nothing compared to how badly I would hurt you if we don't end this."

"Decklan, please."

"This is over, Kimber." He breaks my gaze, crossing the room towards the front door.

"You can't do this. Being with you is my choice."

"And ending it is mine." He rips open the door.

"Decklan." My voice barely breaks the

surface as tears now flow freely down my cheeks.

"Leave, Kimber."

"No." I refuse. "I'm not going to just walk away, I can't."

"You don't have a choice. Now leave." His tone is absolute.

"I'm not leaving."

"I said get the fuck out!" he screams. The slur of the whiskey makes his voice sound so much more vicious than it probably would otherwise. "Now!" I jump when he screams again.

"Please." I am desperate at this point. Fear grips at my chest nearly paralyzing me on the spot.

"So help me god, Kimber, if you don't get the fuck out of my apartment I will remove you from it," he threatens.

"No, you won't," I challenge, tensing when he storms towards me, his hand closing down on my forearm as he pulls me through the room.

"Remember me like this." He forces me onto the landing at the top of the stairs. "And don't ever come back here again." The door slams in my face before I have a chance to say anything.

I stand in front of that door for what feels like an eternity, somehow trying to convince myself that this is all some kind of sick joke and that any moment he's going to open the door and pull me into his arms.

I wait for that moment, but that moment never comes.

Convincing yourself of a truth that your mind refuses to believe is somewhat like falling into a nightmare. Deep down the only way you can cope with it is to make yourself believe it isn't real.

Only this is real...


I don't remember leaving the bar, only the vague memory of someone saying my name as I stepped out onto the sidewalk stuck with me; the drive home's even more of a blur.

It's like one minute I'm standing in front of Decklan's door trying to convince myself none of this is real, the next I am in my dorm with no real recollection of how I got here.

All I know is I feel like the walls are caving in around me and there is no way to survive the weight that is slowly suffocating me.

I can't breathe.

I can't think clearly.

I feel like my heart is literally being torn from my chest, and I am helpless to stop it.

# Chapter Twenty-two

**<u>Decklan</u>**

"You can't keep doing this, dude. I've covered for you for over a week now, but I won't continue to pull your weight." Gavin stares back at me from across the bar, his tone serious. "I know you're going through some shit right now, and I know what next week is..." He pauses, his gaze softening slightly.

"Conner has nothing to do with this," I object, slinging back the remainder of the drink in front of me.

"Conner has everything to do with this," he says, his face hardening, "and you're a fucking idiot if you think he doesn't."

"Watch it," I warn. "You may be my best

friend but that doesn't mean I won't fucking lay you out."

"Really?" He bites, his clear aggravation growing. "Is that how it's going to be now? You're just going to push everyone away this time, including me?"

"I'm not pushing anyone away." Even as I say the words I know deep down they aren't true.

Isn't that exactly what I did to Kimber? Pushed her away? I still can't shake the way she looked at me when I forced her to leave my apartment. I don't think a look has ever fucking gutted me the way that one did.

"You do this every year. Every year when it gets close to the anniversary of the accident you shut down. I've come to expect it, Deck. But this is extreme, even for you. You can't just hole yourself up in that apartment and drink yourself to death. You have friends, a business, and last time I checked a beautiful girl, for reasons unknown to me, who is fucking crazy about you."

"I doubt she'd agree with you there," I mutter, not meeting his gaze.

"Because you fucking discarded her like a piece of fucking trash, Deck." He sighs, running his hands through his hair on a sigh of frustration. "The first girl, dude, the first girl to ever pull you out of the dark fog you've been living in for the past eight years and this is how you treat her?"

"Leave it alone, Gavin." I try to keep my voice controlled.

"No. Look at you. You're fucking miserable. You love that girl and instead of being with her, you're sitting here drowning yourself in the bottom of a bottle. How does that make any sense?"

"Don't fucking pretend like you have any room to talk." I glare back at him.

"What's that supposed to mean?" He hits me with a confused expression.

"Don't you think I know why you never told me about Harlee?" I question. "You didn't want me to know because deep down you have feelings for her. But instead of doing something about it, you ran."

"Feelings for her? I don't even fucking know her," he spits.

"What a cop out." I shake my head. "At least I have the fucking balls to own my shit. You're just a fucking coward."

"And what do you call this, Deck?" He gestures towards me. "Bravery?" His words drip with sarcasm. "Numbing yourself with whiskey while you push away the only girl who you've ever really cared for? I think you're the fucking coward."

"Fuck you, Gavin."

"Fuck you." He spits back at me. "This shit has gone far enough."

"What the fuck are you talking about?" My voice echoes around us.

"You. This incessant need you have to punish yourself. You can't keep blaming yourself for Conner. You can't keep pushing away everyone who cares about you. It's fucking selfish."

"I can do whatever the fuck I want." His comment has my anger hanging on by a mere thread.

"You know what, you're right. But where the fuck are you going to be in five years, hell in ten years for that matter? I'm all about drinking and having a good time, but this isn't what that is, Deck."

"This is my life and it's none of your fucking business, Gavin. Leave it alone," I growl, snagging the bottle in front of me before tilting it over, watching the golden contents splash into my glass.

"None of my business?" He looks at me like he's in disbelief. "None of my fucking business," he repeats, shaking his head slowly side to side.

"That's what I said," I confirm coldly.

"So I guess the fact that I co-own this bar and am doing all the work is none of my business. The fact that I am your best friend, and I'm watching you spiral down a dark hole I'm not sure you will be able to find your way out of, is none of my business. The fact that my brother, my family, is throwing away his chance to be happy, I guess that's none of my business, too." He snags the bottle from the bar and drops it onto the back counter.

"You're fucking killing yourself, Deck." He seethes, staring daggers at me.

"Good," I snap, pouring the contents of the glass down my throat before slamming it onto the bar.

"Get your shit together or I'm cutting your ass out," he threatens.

"You can't do that." I let out a dark laugh.

"Like hell I can't. The lease of this building is in my name. The business loan is in my name." He reminds me. "I don't want to do this with you, Deck, I really don't. But I also won't continue to do all the work while you drink yourself fucking stupid. Get. Your. Shit. Together." He emphasizes each word. "Or I'm done. I've spent enough of my life picking your ass up, it's time you learn how to do it yourself."

"Fuck you," I spit. "Cut me out. See if I fucking care."

Standing, I shove the bar stool violently, letting it crash to the floor before spinning and walking away. Gavin yells after me, but his voice is muffled and fogged by the liquor running through my veins and the amount of distance I have already put between us.

Shoving my way outside, I immediately reach for the pack of cigarettes that are shoved into the front pocket of my jeans, dropping the pack twice before finally managing to get a cigarette out.

Pressing it between my lips I light it, taking a deep inhale as I slide down onto the curb that sits just feet from the front entrance of the bar.

Who the fuck does he think he is?

Anger seethes through my blood, my hand shaking slightly as I lift the cigarette to my lips and take another deep inhale.

"It's a bit early isn't it?" I hear a soft voice behind me.

I turn to the left just in time to see a petite red head slide down next to me.

"Aubrey," I say, surprised that I even remember her name. I'd say the main reason I do is because she is the last person I slept with before Kimber.

"What are you doing here?" I turn my face forward, taking another hit of my cigarette.

"I just finished meeting my sister for lunch." She gestures across the street. "What about you? What are you doing out here?"

"What does it fucking look like?" I bite, ignoring the sharp inhale that sounds from her mouth at my words.

"Everything okay?" She rests her hand

against my back, my body going ridged beneath her touch.

I barely know this girl. I don't know why she feels like she has the right to push her way into my shit. Just because I fucked her doesn't mean were friends.

"Fucking perfect." I blow out a stream of thick smoke.

"Yeah I can tell." She laughs nervously. "You need a shoulder?" she tacks on.

I know her game. I can tell by the way her hand slides across my back that she would like to be much more than a shoulder, and honestly, I'm considering the notion myself.

The thought of burying myself inside her tight little body and forgetting this fucking life for a few minutes sounds more appealing than I expect it to. I would say the whiskey plays a huge role in that thought process, but I don't have it me to care.

"Just a shoulder?" I turn my gaze towards her, watching the way her eyes darken as she bites down gently on her bottom lip.

"Or whatever else you need." Her voice drops low.

"Fuck it." I flip my cigarette into the street before standing, pulling Aubrey up with me.

She's all too eager to follow me inside the bar and as much as I know I shouldn't be doing this, a part of me feels like maybe I need to. Maybe if I fuck someone else I will be able to forget about Kimber.

Just the thought of her name causes a tight knot to settle into the pit of my stomach.

Shaking it off, I ignore Gavin's eyes on us as I lead Aubrey through the door that goes up to my apartment, dragging her up the stairs behind me. I don't fucking care what he thinks; he has no right to fucking judge anyone.

Throwing open my door, Aubrey is on me before I even step over the threshold. I stumble backward slightly into the apartment, swallowing down the sick feeling that creeps into my throat when her lips connect with mine.

I try to push it away, shake off how wrong it feels to kiss her but I can't. It only gets worse as she unbuttons her shirt and drops it to the floor, her hands skirting across my stomach as she reaches underneath my t-shirt.

Backing her into the support beam that runs through the middle of the room, my mind immediately flashes to the last time I pinned Kimber against it, how I felt her bare around me, the way her body trembled beneath my touch.

Breaking away from Aubrey's mouth, the moment my eyes trace her across her flesh, I reach down and stop her hands from unzipping my pants.

"What's wrong?" She pants, dropping her mouth to my neck.

You're not her, is all I can think but refrain from saying.

"Stop," I say, my voice lost somewhere in my throat. "Stop," I repeat more forcefully, grabbing her shoulders to hold her firm as I take a step back. "Just stop." I pant, furious with myself for even considering doing this or even thinking that I could for that matter.

Everything about this feels wrong. Fuck me.

Here I have a beautiful girl throwing herself at me, one I know is a good fuck, and I can't even fucking get hard. I can't kiss her without thinking of Kimber's lips. I can't look at her without thinking of Kimber's body. While this girl may be attractive, she has nothing on the woman who controls my body and my heart.

"I'm sorry, I can't do this." I take another step backward, not missing the hurt expression that crosses her features.

"Seriously?" Her tone shifts from soft and sweet to angry in the matter of a second.

"You should go." I reach down, retrieving her shirt from the floor.

Extending my hand out, she looks down at the article of clothing and then back up to my face not trying at all to hide her confusion.

She opens her mouth to speak but then snaps it closed, clearly deciding against whatever it is she wants to say. Snagging the shirt from my hand, she's out of the apartment before she even has it all the way on, slamming the door violently behind her.

I stare at that door for what feels like an eternity, my inebriated state causing me to fixate on that one object. I can still hear Kimber's voice, the way she pleaded with me not to do this as I forced her out of that very door.

I pushed her away...just like I've pushed everyone away.

I find clarity in the moment, as if somehow the fog has temporarily been lifted and I can see clearly for the first time in a very long time.

I think about Conner, about the accident, about how badly I wanted to switch places with him, about how badly I still do. I think about my mom, how she could barely look at me for weeks following the accident.

Over and over the moments play through my mind, stirring emotions inside of me that I have long since kept buried. Emotions that I feared would consume me if I gave into them.

Kimber is the only thing that has ever given me any kind of peace; a bright light that cut through the thick darkness I buried myself in for years. She's the only thing that makes any sense to me anymore.

I was so focused on not hurting her that I couldn't see just how badly I was hurting her. I just don't know if that's something I can come back from. I don't even know if I could bring myself to try.

Gavin's right, I'm miserable without her but that doesn't change the fact that I will never be the kind of man that deserves her love.

Letting her go is the only way I know how to show her just how much she means to me. I want more for her, better. No matter how badly I want her, deep down I know I did the right thing. I choose to put her happiness over my own.

I just hope one day I can find a way to live with that choice.

# Chapter Twenty-three

## <u>Kimber</u>

"Are you gonna get that?" Harlee hollers from the bathroom as I sit cross-legged on top of my bed, trying my best to focus on the dry reading material of my textbook and not on the rapid knocking that has been sounding against our door for the past thirty seconds.

"It's your date, why do I have to get it?" I whine, hating how pathetic I sound.

"Please, Kimber, I'm not ready," she pleads through the closed door.

"Fine." I huff, pushing up off the bed.

I adjust my black leggings and pull down my long gray sweater before taking one quick look at myself in the mirror. Considering I've been holed up in here all afternoon studying, I don't look half bad. Well, other than the fact that my hair is tied up in the messiest bun ever and you can clearly see traces of dark circles under my eyes from my inability to sleep.

Letting out a deep sigh, I shake away the thoughts of Decklan that immediately creep into my mind. It's been nearly a week since I last saw him. I wish I could say it's gotten easier but if I'm being truthful, it's actually gotten much worse.

"I'm coming," I yell when the rapid knocking starts again after just a few seconds.

Crossing the space of the room, I rip open the door, only half looking at who's on the other side considering Harlee is expecting Bryan. It takes a few seconds for my brain to register that's not who it is, and I immediately do a double take.

"Gavin?" I question, taking a step backward into the room as he pushes his way inside. "Harlee is busy," I say, assuming that's why he's here.

"This isn't about Harlee." He closes the door before spinning towards me, his blue eyes filled with concern. "It's about Decklan."

The mere mention of his name sends my heart galloping inside my chest and causes the sickest feeling to knot in the pit of my stomach.

"Decklan?" I barely get his name out, the last part catching in my throat.

"Look, I wouldn't have come here if I didn't think it was the only way," he says, apology lining his features.

"What is it?" I blurt, wishing he would just spit it out already. "Is Decklan okay?" Fear cripples my insides.

"He's fine, physically anyways." He sighs, running a hand through his short brown hair. "Emotionally, well let's just say I've never seen him so low. He's barely left his apartment in a week, he's completely dropped all of his responsibilities at the bar, and at the rate he's going he will have eliminated our entire stock of whiskey by week's end. I know he's pushing you away, hell he's pushing everyone away, it's what he does. But I need you to not let him. If he succeeds in losing you, I'm not sure he'll recover."

I open my mouth to respond but before I can get a word out Harlee emerges from the bathroom, the wide smile on her face immediately fading when she sees it's Gavin in our room and not Bryan.

"What the hell are you doing here?" she bites, her harsh voice not hiding the glimmer of excitement that lights behind her eyes.

"I'm here for Kimber." His voice remains clipped as he does his best not to look at her, only throwing her a brief glance before turning his attention back to me.

"As I was saying, I need your help," he continues.

"What's going on?" Harlee immediately interjects, crossing the small space towards me.

"This doesn't have anything to do with you." He finally meets her gaze, his forehead creasing in frustration.

"The hell it doesn't," she snaps. "Kimber is my friend. If there's something going on, I have the right to know."

"It's fine," I interject, pulling Gavin's attention back to me, gesturing for him to continue.

"Look, I can't explain everything." He lets out a loud exhale. "There's something you don't know about Decklan, something he's chosen to keep from you. In order to understand what you're dealing with, I feel like you need to know the whole story."

"Okay..." I draw out, waiting for him to continue.

"Can I explain on the way?" he asks, surprising me.

"On the way to where?" I question, not trying to hide my confusion.

"To the cemetery." He steps towards the door, tearing it open.

"The cemetery?" I stutter.

"Where Decklan's brother is buried.

Now can we go?" he asks impatiently from the open doorway.

I don't try to hide my surprise over his statement. I didn't know Decklan had a brother that died, though now that I think about it, it makes sense. The comments Trey made, the way Decklan would shut down when I tried to find out more about his family, the rift that was so clearly preventing him from having any kind of real relationship with his mom.

I can't deny that a part of me feels very hurt that he didn't feel like he could share something like this with me. Then again, in a way I kind of understand why he didn't.

"I'm coming, too." Harlee breaks into my thoughts, grabbing her jacket from the hook next to the door. "It's not up for discussion." She stops Gavin before he can object.

"What about your date?" I question, stepping into my boots before sliding my own jacket on.

"Date?" I can tell by the expression on Gavin's face he doesn't mean to say it out loud.

It's clear Harlee can see that as well. She looks at him for a long moment before finally turning her attention back to me.

"I'll text him in the car, it's fine. No way I'm gonna let you go alone."

"She's not alone." Gavin waits until we are both in the hall before pulling the door closed.

Ignoring his comment, Harlee links her arm through mine, clearly seeing that I need the additional support right now. I'm already a mess from the last couple of weeks, now to have Gavin show up so out of the blue and tell me Decklan is in some kind of trouble, my poor mind is having trouble keeping up.

We reach Gavin's truck that's parked just outside the dorm building in no time. Harlee insists that I ride in the middle so she doesn't have to sit next to him. The tension between these two is off the charts. Even in my fog-like state, I can see it plain as day.

I wait until Gavin has pulled out of the parking lot and is speeding down the road before finally pinning my eyes on the side of his face.

"Now are you going to tell me what the hell is going on?" I ask, feeling like I might split apart from the anticipation of not knowing what he's going to say or how it may or may not change the way I feel about Decklan.

It's clear that whatever it is, it's bad. Otherwise, Gavin wouldn't be so hesitant to tell me, and Decklan wouldn't have chosen to keep it from me for that matter.

My stomach flutters with nerves as

Gavin opens his mouth and starts to speak. He gets only five words out before I stop hearing him. A rush of emotion hits me like a tidal wave, pulling me under its crippling weight, inhibiting my ability to hear, to breathe, to process the information I'm being presented with.

I never knew heartbreak until Decklan forced me out of his life. But now...now I know heartbreak beyond my own. Because right now my heart is breaking all over again, only this time, it's breaking for Decklan, not because of him.

****

By the time we reach the cemetery the sun has almost set, a low orange glow now filling the evening sky. Gavin tells me where I can find Conner's grave but says he thinks it's best if he and Harlee hang back.

My heart is beating so loudly against my rib cage as I make my way through the cemetery, I swear even the dead can hear it.

I finally spot Decklan along the back row of grave sites, my feet faltering the moment I see him. He's sitting on the ground, his knees pulled into his chest, his head down. It takes everything I have to force my legs to work, to make my body move towards him.

"Decklan?" I stop just a couple feet

behind where's he sitting in front of his brother's headstone; *Conner Roderick Taylor January, 3 1994-November 29, 2008* scrawled across the front in the perfect font.

Today's date... November 29.

His shoulders tense the moment my weak voice registers, but he doesn't turn to face me. Several long silent moments pass between us; him unable to speak, me too afraid to move any closer.

"What are you doing here?" When his voice finally filters through the silence, it's broken and riddled with emotion. It would be enough to break my heart again if it wasn't already splintered into a million different pieces.

"Gavin." I know he doesn't need any additional explanation. "He's worried about you."

"He doesn't need to be." His response is cold, distant.

"I'm worried about you," I add.

"Please don't." I can hear the emotion clog his throat, and it takes everything I have to remain at a distance.

"Tell me what happened. Tell me about Conner." I take a couple steps forward, stopping just a foot behind him.

"Tell me, Decklan," I request softly when he makes no attempt to answer me.

"He was a great kid." His voice breaks in

the middle. "He was three years younger than me, only fourteen." He stops abruptly, his shoulders trembling slightly.

"Keep going." I slide down next to him, my eyes focused on the stone in front of us.

"He used to follow me everywhere." He finally continues after a long moment. "He always had to tag along no matter what I was doing. I used to hate it." He lets out an emotion filled laugh. "I remember just wishing he would leave me the hell alone."

"Tell me what happened to him, Decklan." I finally chance a peek in his direction, my stomach bottoming out the moment I register his flushed tear-stained face.

It's one thing to see a man cry, it's something else entirely to see a man like Decklan cry. Tears immediately form at the back of my eyes, and I blink rapidly trying to will them away.

He wipes at his cheeks with the back of his hands, his gaze remaining firmly in front of him. Every fiber of my being wants to wrap him in my arms and comfort him, but I refrain, knowing right now it would likely make things worse.

"I tried to get him to stay home. I told him he was too young for the type of shit that went on at Paxton's parties, but he wouldn't take no for an answer. I could never hold my ground with that kid." He smiles, but it's a painfully gut-wrenching combination of happiness over the memory of his brother and devastation over what he knows comes next.

"I was fucking with the radio. I should have seen the stop sign. I'd driven that road hundreds of times before, I knew it was there, yet somehow on that night, I ran straight through it. A truck approaching from the right hit the passenger side of my car going around fifty miles an hour according to the police report. I don't remember it. I don't remember anything. Just the crack of my head on the driver's side window and the sound of shattering glass and crunching metal." He takes a deep shaky breath, clearly trying to hold himself together.

"When I woke up there were people everywhere. Voices filtered all around me, but I only recognized one: my mother's." A pained sob escapes his throat, a fresh onset of tears falling down his cheeks.

"She was on her way home from work and came upon the accident. She recognized my car I guess. I don't really know. All I remember is hearing her scream. It was loud. That's when I knew."

"I killed him, Kimber." He turns his tear-filled bloodshot eyes on me, the pain behind them almost more than I can bear.

I don't realize I'm crying too until he

reaches over and gently brushes my cheekbone with the pad of his thumb. The gesture only makes me cry harder. Even in this very vulnerable moment, he's still worried about taking care of me.

"You can't blame yourself." My words are weak and broken.

"But don't you see, it's my fault. It all could have been avoided. Conner is dead because of me." He drops his hand away from my face, turning back towards his brother's grave. "I have nothing left, nothing but his fading memory and the fucking headaches that refuse to let me forget what I've done."

"I'm so fucking sorry," he cries, dropping his head down as sobs rack through his entire body. "I'm so fucking sorry," he repeats, rocking slightly back and forth as despair rips through him.

Before I even realize I've moved, I'm on my knees, wrapping my arms around his shoulders as I pull his head into my chest, my body rocking with his as I fight to comfort him. Resting my cheek on the top of his head, I hold him tightly, the feeling of his body trembling beneath mine the most gut-wrenching thing I've ever experienced.

I try to hold my own emotions in, to be strong for him, but feeling this man that I once viewed as unbreakable crumble beneath me is more than I can take. It rips me apart; a pain like I've never felt before.

This must be what it means to truly love someone; you take their pain as your own and you share the burden.

"This isn't your fault," I finally manage to say after several long moments. "You can't keep blaming yourself for this. Accidents happen every day, Decklan. Conner died, but that doesn't mean you did. He would want you to live. Live your life for the both of you." I loosen my grip, rocking back on my knees as I turn his face upwards to meet mine.

"I understand why you pushed me away. And it's okay. I understand. But I also need to say something, and you're going to listen to me." I push his messy hair away from his face. "You are worthy of love, Decklan Taylor. You deserve it, even if you can't see that yet. And I won't give up on you. I will just have to love you for the both of us until you can find a way to love yourself as well."

"I can't." He takes a deep breath, wiping at his cheeks.

"Yes, you can. You can forgive yourself. You will forgive yourself. And I will be here with you every step of the way." I cup his face in my hands. "Because I love you that much."

"I don't deserve your love." His bloodshot gray eyes hold my gaze.

"Yes you do," I reassure him. "You deserve to be loved; you just have to let me do it. Nothing will bring Conner back." I drop my hands away from his face, sinking down further to sit eye level with him on the ground. "But you can honor him every day by living the life he never got."

"I don't know how," he admits.

"Then I'll help you." I give him a weak smile.

"I'm sorry... for everything."

"Don't." I shake my head. "You don't have to apologize."

"I'm so in love with you that it terrifies me." He reaches out, running his thumb along my bottom lip.

"I'm so in love with you that it terrifies me," I repeat his statement back to him before leaning down and pressing my lips gently to his.

# Chapter Twenty-four

## **<u>Decklan</u>**

"I'm sorry," I finally mutter the words I came all this way to say, looking up to find my mother's tear-filled eyes staring back at me.

"Oh my dear boy, you have nothing to apologize for." She reaches across the table, taking my hand in hers. "You are my son, and I love you."

"I was just so angry. I didn't understand how you could ever forgive me."

"There was nothing to forgive. It was an accident and accidents happen. I was devastated over losing your brother, but never once did I blame you." The kindness in her eyes is enough to fucking gut me right here.

All the shit I put her through, how awful of a son I've been since Conner's death, I just don't understand how she can so easily dismiss that behavior.

"I loved Conner, just as I love you and Trey," she continues. "Losing him was like losing a part of myself, and I knew from that moment on I would never be the same. But that didn't mean that my love for you changed. If anything, it became stronger."

"I was so awful to you."

"You were angry, and you were in pain. I understood that. I tried to make you see that I didn't blame you, but you were so convinced I did that you only saw what you wanted to see. It killed me to watch you punish yourself, to withdraw and push everyone away. It was almost like I lost two sons that night." She swipes at a stray tear that trickles slowly down her cheek.

"I'm sorry," I apologize again, not sure what else to say.

What else can I say after eight years?

"Do not apologize to me again." She shakes her head, squeezing my hand. "I just want you to be happy."

"I'm working on that." I give her a soft smile.

"What's her name?" Her lips turn up in a knowing grin. "What? You think your old mother doesn't recognize a woman's touch when I see one?" She laughs at the confused look on my face.

"Kimber." The mere mention of her

name brings a smile to my lips.

"So when do I get to meet her?"

\*\*\*\*

Driving across town to pick Kimber up from work, I feel almost weightless. The heavy burden I have carried with me for so long lifting dramatically by making peace with my past and with my mom.

Nothing happens overnight, and I know that I will have good days and bad, but for the first time since I was a teenager, I feel something other than my pain and grief. I feel hope.

Pulling my bike off to the side of the road, I kill the engine and climb off, depositing my helmet onto the seat. I spot Kimber before I even make it across the street. She's almost completely visible through the floor to ceiling glass wall that separates the outdoor patio from the indoor restaurant.

I stop just outside and watch her for a long moment; her blonde hair tied up in a messy knot, a few loose pieces falling around her face. She has to be the most beautiful creature I have ever laid my eyes on.

She looks up from wiping off the table in front of her and catches my eyes, a huge smile stretching across her face. Holding up her index finger, she gestures to give her a minute before disappearing from view.

Within moments she reappears, pushing up on her tip toes to lay a kiss on my mouth the instant she reaches me.

"I missed you," she speaks against my lips. "How'd it go?" She backs away, tangling her fingers with mine.

"Really well," I admit, pulling her back to me. "Thank you." I drop another brief kiss to her mouth before pulling back to meet her gaze.

"For what?" She smiles sweetly up at me, the action fucking melting me on the spot.

Fuck me. I'm a goner.

"For believing that I'm worth forgiving." I tuck a loose strand of hair behind her ear, my hand lingering against her cheek. "I love you."

"And I love you." She turns her face inward, kissing the palm of my hand.

"It's a good thing too because you're not getting rid of me." I lean forward and kiss her forehead.

"Oh man." She sighs out playfully. "I guess I'll just have to find a way to deal with it." She laughs when I abruptly squeeze her side.

"And I hope you're free next Saturday because we're meeting my mother for lunch," I add on, watching her eyes widen. "She's dying to meet you."

"You told her about me?" She almost seems surprised by this.

"I did," I confirm. "So Saturday?"

"I'll be there." She pushes up and presses her lips to mine again. "But first, you have to go somewhere with me." She pulls back and hits me with excited eyes.

"Now?"

"Right now." She laughs, grabbing my hand as she drags me towards my motorcycle.

\*\*\*\*

## Kimber

"Where are we?" Decklan asks as he climbs off his motorcycle and looks up at the large brick building in front of him.

"You'll see." I reach out to tangle my fingers with his. "Come on," I say, leading him towards the front entrance.

"What is this place?" he asks, pulling open the door before following me inside.

"It's the art lab," I explain, leading him down the main corridor to the last door at the end of the hall. "It's where I've been practically living this past couple of weeks." I give him a sweet smile before pushing my way inside the lab room I've been working in.

He follows silently behind me through the large bright room, various pieces of half-finished art lining multiple easels and large sections of the walls. With final projects due next week, it's a wonder there's no one here tonight. Most nights that I've been here there have been several other students here as well.

I lead Decklan to the far corner of the room, most of my supplies still spread out on my workstation from last night.

"I finally finished my project." I turn towards him, coming to a stop next the easel that is turned inward facing the wall.

"The self-portrait?" he asks, having heard me speak of it a few times before.

I nod. After everything that's happened over the past few weeks, I thought maybe showing him this would reassure just how much he means to me.

"I want you to see it." I give him a small smile before turning the easel to face him.

I don't look at the painting; I already know what's there. Instead, I study his reaction, the way his eyes scan the canvas, a slow smiling pulling at the corners of his mouth.

"Wow." The word is barely a whisper as his gaze meets mine.

"It's us," I say, for the first time turning to face the painting.

The scattered colors and lines came together more perfectly than I envisioned, but I guess that's what happens when you paint with your heart instead of your head. My smile widens as I stare back at my creation; two faces blended as one. One side is my face, the other Decklan's, the background swirled with the most brilliant reds.

"I realized the reason I couldn't paint a portrait of how I viewed myself was because I didn't truly know myself. At least not until I met you. You not only showed me who I am, you became a part of me." I flick my eyes back towards him.

"It's incredible." He reaches for me, pulling me into his arms. "You're incredible." He breathes, dropping his mouth to mine. "And I'm never going to let you go again." He pulls back, his face hovering just inches from mine.

"Good, because I never want you to." I push up, wrapping my arms around his neck as I press my lips once again to his.

Falling in love with a man like Decklan Taylor wasn't just crazy, it was downright stupid, but I know with complete certainty that I wouldn't change it for anything. Because no matter how crazy or how stupid it is, at the end of the day it's love.

It's our love.

*Crazy, stupid, incredible, life-altering love.*

*The End*

## *<u>Crazy Stupid Love Playlist</u>*

*A special thank you to each of these amazing artists. So much of my inspiration for Crazy Stupid Love came from this playlist.*

*Love on the Brain- Rihanna*
*Ride- Chase Rice*
*Taciturn- Stone Sour*
*Remedy- Adele*
*Say You Love Me- Jessie Ware*
*Fall into Me- Brantley Gilbert*
*Incomplete- James Bay*
*Sea of Lovers- Christina Perri*
*The Way I Was- Aubrey Peeples*
*Over and Over- Nathan Sykes*
*Hollow- Tori Kelly*
*Writing's On the Wall- Sam Smith*
*I Can't Go On Without You- Kaleo*